# an off year

# an off year

## claire zulkey

DISCARD dutton

DUTTON BOOKS

A *member of* Penguin Group (USA) Inc

Published by the Penguin Group

Penguin Group (USA) Inc., 375 Hudson Street, New York, New York 10014, U.S.A. • Penguin Group (Canada), 90 Eglinton Avenue East, Suite 700, Toronto, Ontario M4P 2Y3, Canada (a division of Pearson Penguin Canada Inc.) • Penguin Books Ltd, 80 Strand, London WC2R 0RL, England • Penguin Ireland, 25 St Stephen's Green, Dublin 2, Ireland (a division of Penguin Books Ltd) • Penguin Group (Australia), 250 Camberwell Road, Camberwell, Victoria 3124, Australia (a division of Pearson Australia Group Pty Ltd) • Penguin Books India Pvt Ltd, 11 Community Centre, Panchsheel Park, New Delhi–110 017, India • Penguin Group (NZ), 67 Apollo Drive, Rosedale, North Shore 0632, New Zealand (a division of Pearson New Zealand Ltd) • Penguin Books (South Africa) (Pty) Ltd, 24 Sturdee Avenue, Rosebank, Johannesburg 2196, South Africa • Penguin Books Ltd, Registered Offices: 80 Strand, London WC2R 0RL, England

The publisher does not have any control over and does not assume any responsibility for author or third-party websites or their content.

CIP Data is available.

Published in the United States by Dutton Books,
a member of Penguin Group (USA) Inc.
345 Hudson Street, New York, New York 10014
www.penguin.com/youngreaders

*Designed by Liz Frances*

Printed in USA      First Edition
ISBN 978-0-525-42159-7      10 9 8 7 6 5 4 3 2 1

*To my husband, Steve Delahoyde.*
*I would have dedicated this to you even if you hadn't told me to.*

# an off year

# august

**I raised the key** and hesitated. Something wasn't right. I turned around. "You know, actually, I think I'm just going to go back home with you," I told my dad, who was still trying to decipher the campus map.

"What?"

"Yeah. I'm not going to stay here tonight."

He blinked and folded up the map. Incorrectly. "Wait, I'm confused. Are you saying you want to get a hotel for the night or something?"

"No. We're going home. Now."

"We?" he said. "You mean as in 'not just me'? The two of us?"

"That's right," I said.

"What?" he asked again.

A dry erase board with a marker clipped to it was stuck to the door. I picked up the marker and wrote to the girl who would have been my roommate: "Molly, sorry, I won't be here after all. Have a good year. Sincerely, Cecily." The ink was a happy fuchsia color, fun for a fun girls' dorm room. Oh well.

I took a deep breath and faced Dad, preparing to be screamed at, ready to be told that there was no way in hell I was going home with him. This was new territory for us: I'd never really done anything like this, so I had no idea how he'd react. I was going to stand my ground, though, and keep calmly repeating my plan: I was not going to college today. I wasn't sure why this was the plan, but this was the plan, and I was sticking to it. If he didn't let me back in the car with him, I was prepared to walk back to Chicago. It would take many days, but I was wearing a comfortable pair of Chuck Taylors. I felt a little bit giddy. And also a little like I was going to throw up.

Dad stood for a moment, not looking angry, but pensive, like he was looking for the right word in the crossword puzzle. Across the hall, a mother and her daughter, both redheads, screamed at each other about how to put together the dresser they had bought at Target.

He looked down at the map in his hand for a moment, as if it might give us some information. I was dying to refold it for him. "Um, may I ask why?"

I shrugged and shook my head. "It's just . . . it's not . . . I can't. I just seriously can't." I was having a hard time making a complete sentence. My brain had a perfectly articulated argument, but it hadn't reached my mouth yet. I paused for a second and willed it to flow out, but it obviously hadn't totally formed. So I shrugged.

Dad fixed his bluish-gray eyes on me, but I couldn't really look him in the eye because of the glare of the irritating fluorescent hallway lights off his glasses. "Cecily . . . are you sure? You don't want to sleep on it?"

"No. I'm absolutely sure."

"You—" Dad started to say something but stopped, and for some reason gazed down at the horrible industrial carpeting under our feet that I didn't intend to look at for much longer. It was chocolate brown with flecks of yellow in it, probably to hide years of embedded dirt. Dad adjusted his glasses, ran a hand through the short, still mostly dark curls on his head, then put his hand in his pocket and took out the car keys. "All right." He hesitated for a second. *Here it comes,* I thought. "If you're sure, then. Do you want to go home now or get some lunch?" he asked.

"We can get lunch on the way." I was making decisive judgment calls all over the place.

We walked back to the car, past crowds of kids and parents rushing through the halls and the parking lot with boxes and trash bags full of clothes, all hugging and crying and yelling at one another. We got back in the car and drove west, putting Gambier, Ohio, behind us, stopping at an Arby's in Indiana to eat. I had a roast beef sandwich. I offered to drive at one point, but Dad just shook his head. It was pretty awkward, but I'd been through worse. I ignored the silence in the car and drowned out the questions in my head by reading each billboard we saw and imagining what they'd sound like if read in different accents.

We didn't say anything until we got home many hours later. We drove back into Chicago, got off the expressway, and headed east, turning onto our little street, which stretched along a short Lake Michigan beach. The sun began to set over the backyards—it was barely starting to rise when we left.

"Cecily, what about your stuff?" asked Dad as I closed the car door and headed to the house from the garage. My head hurt from watching the miles of cookie-cutter homes that bordered the highway on the drive back. I was glad to be back in our solid old redbrick house where things felt right again.

"I'll get it in a bit," I said.

"So you're bringing it all in?"

"What else am I going to do with it?" I asked. Meaning, *No, in case you're wondering, we're not going back tomorrow.*

When we walked in, my brother, Josh, stood in the kitchen cutting a sandwich in half on top of a paper napkin. Our cleaning lady, Yolanda, had come while we were gone, and the room smelled like Fantastik. Josh was leaving for school in a few days himself, to start his junior year in Madison.

"Hi," he said, glancing toward us, and then did an actual double take, the kind you usually only see in the movies. "Wait. Aren't you supposed to not be here?" he asked me. Dad didn't say anything, just put his keys away in a drawer and went to the refrigerator to get a pop, so I would have to do the talking.

"I didn't want to go," I said, as if I had walked out of a movie I didn't like. Superhero, our black regal-looking-but-often-silly Belgian shepherd, ran up to me, and I got down on my knees for hugs. "Hello, Mister Man!" I cried. Here was a perfectly good reason not to go to college: my dog wouldn't have it.

"Why?" Josh asked, taking a big mouthful of his sandwich, leaning against the counter in his mesh gym shorts and flip-flops, getting crumbs on the formerly perfect white linoleum.

"Is that roast beef?" I asked.

"Yeah."

"I had roast beef, too. Arby's."

"Nice. But why didn't you want to go? What's going on?"

I shrugged and retied my ponytail. The heat and humidity and general excitement of the day had styled the shorter curls around my head into a mini 'fro. Josh widened his eyes, looking at Dad and then back at me. It was that I-see-something-serious-is-going-on-but-I'll-get-the-details-later face. I tried to catch his eye, but he examined the ceiling, his eyebrows almost disappearing under his dark mop of hair. With nothing else to say, I started upstairs to my room, then suddenly realized that I had no idea what I would do when I got there. I was beginning to wonder if this was such a good idea after all. But it felt like it was the only choice. I had to pretend to know what I was doing for a little while—until I actually did.

"Cecily," Dad said before I reached the landing. I turned around and looked down at him. "Somebody is going to have to unload the car." He sounded normal, like he was asking me to get groceries out of the trunk after a trip to the Jewel.

"I'll do it in a little bit," I said. I scrambled upstairs before I could hear Dad and Josh talking about me.

In the hall, I ran into my older sister, Germaine. Not literally, although we had spent the summer purposefully bumping shoulders when we walked past each other from our rooms on opposite ends of the hall, an unsubtle reminder that the house wasn't big enough for the two of us. Germaine had graduated from college just a few months earlier and was living at home, sort of looking for a job, sort of not. Germaine and I had never been great friends. I had hoped that being away at college would mellow her out, but instead she got even more irritable than she was before she left. She seemed to hate being at home with us; she usually sequestered herself in her room or went out with her boyfriend, or sat at the computer listening to bitter pseudofeminist pop through headphones while she e-mailed her friends about how much her life sucked. I didn't know why she didn't just leave.

Our household was sort of divided up into Team Mom and Team Dad. Germaine was on Team Mom; she looked like her (dirty blond hair, squinty blue eyes) and, like Mom, didn't really want to be around us. Josh and I, meanwhile, had Dad's dark curly hair and gray (sometimes blue or greenish) eyes. I put up with Germaine because I had to; I believed she was the negative energy in the house. Mom was sort of no energy; she hadn't lived at home since she and Dad divorced when I was eleven.

"What are you doing here?" Germaine asked. She smelled like coconuts and magazine perfume samples, which probably meant she had been tanning earlier. She flipped some long blond hair over her shoulder. She'd gotten her hair done recently, too. Busy day.

"What are *you* doing here?"

"I live here," she said. "You're supposed to be in school."

"Surprise!" I said, heading into my room. "They decided I was so brilliant they just automatically graduated me." She snorted and went downstairs to get the whole story. I shut the door and lay down on the hot-pink carpet that I loathed and yet spent an inordinate amount of time on. My mother had cruelly picked it out and had it installed for me one summer while I was away at camp. I'm not sure why she thought I'd like the color of pink Lava lamps, but it was also insanely soft, so I tried to pretend it was actually magenta so I wouldn't throw up when I was in the room. After pulling out my ponytail holder so that my hair spread out around my head in a tangle on the floor, I stretched out on my back and watched the fading sunlight slant by on the butter-colored walls. My mind raced with terrifying worries about what was going to come next, yet my body felt calm and peaceful, which was extra confusing.

*Holy shit,* I thought. *I can't believe I just did that. What now?*

After about a half hour of me lying around like that, Dad called me to come down and help bring the boxes in from the car; he must have been explaining what had gone down to Josh and Germaine. I knew I'd be able to stall for about ten minutes before he really started getting fed up with asking me. That was how it usually was, anyway. Dad and I got along fine most of the time, as long as I did what he asked in a timely manner. And even when I did get in trouble, we'd be joking about it soon after. Like, every once in a while, I'd get home late after hanging out with my friend Kate, and it would go something like this: I came upstairs to find Dad in the leather chair in the living room, reading some nine-hundred-page manuscript he was editing.

He'd say: "It's late, Cecily. You should have called."

"Oh, I just wanted to make my arrival home a surprise."

"And what a horrible surprise it's turned out to be. I was thinking I was finally free of you. How's Kate?" And then I'd tell him that she'd grown a third arm and was still figuring out how to use it to her advantage, and he'd say that was nice, and I'd kiss him good night and go to bed.

As we'd stood there in the freshman dorm, I suppose Dad could have said, "The hell you're not going to school," shoved me in the room, and run back to his car. But that wasn't really his style. He was mellow. A history professor, not a shover.

But I didn't know what he was thinking at this particular moment. I didn't want to push it and risk getting yelled at/ thrown out of the house/murdered for something as minor as boxes. But I really didn't want to go downstairs, since I still didn't have a good explanation as to why I had made that one split-second decision earlier that day. When I left that morning, I hadn't felt scared or sad about leaving Dad. I'd felt pretty ready. But, staring at that dorm-room door, something just didn't feel right.

It was strange. I never got that homesick, either, after all those summers spent at camp or trudging after Mom in Europe. Sure, I was close to Dad, but not won't-go-to-college close. Before he could give me a second warning about the boxes, the phone rang. Dad yelled, "Cecily! It's your mother!"

I sighed and walked down the stairs as slowly as possible.

"Why would you do a thing like that?" she asked with no greeting as soon as I picked up the phone on the kitchen table. Dad was rinsing some cherry tomatoes in a colander for dinner, his back to me.

Apparently I didn't need to break the good news to Mom myself. I put the phone against my shoulder and sat down on the terra-cotta floor to give Superhero some tummy rubbing.

"I don't know."

"Huh," she said, sounding distracted. I heard laughter in the background.

"Where are you right now?" I asked. Mom rarely called from the same city twice in a row.

"Florence. It's fabulous. Anyway, that sounds like something I would have done at your age. You know, spur of the moment. These gap years are really the thing to do, apparently—a lot of my friends' children are doing it lately, from what I hear."

"Awesome." I was surprised to hear that she was friends with other parents, let alone discussed child rearing with them.

"Well. You know, you should do something amazing if you're taking time off, like write a book or learn to paint or something. . . . Listen, I need to get going. Maybe if you want, you can meet me here or later in Portugal," she said in her cool, crisp voice. It sounded like a horrifying idea. Mom technically lived in Miami, but she was constantly traveling, for no particular reason, with no particular guy.

"No, thanks. Not now."

"Well, have fun," she said. "Bye." And then a click. Mom hung up first, always. I put the phone on the cradle, a waste of conversation. Obviously all of this wasn't important enough to merit a trip back to flyover country. When Mom came for my high school graduation, all she did was show up for the ceremony, which isn't a special family moment when it's held in a twenty-thousand-seat stadium and you're the five hundredth out of seven hundred people in your class to graduate. She stayed for a three-mimosa lunch at the Cheesecake Factory, and then she was off to catch a connection to Maui.

With the phone put away and nobody talking to me, I had nothing left to do but check out the unpacking situation. The boxes I was supposed to unload had miraculously reappeared in the kitchen, stacked next to the stairs. Maybe if I waited long enough, whatever magical elves had transported them from the car to the kitchen would then spirit them up to my bedroom and back into the closet, where I could reorganize everything the way it was supposed to be. Right now my closet stood sad and empty, with a few skeletal hangers rattling around inside.

The kitchen radio played the White Sox game. Germaine and I didn't care about baseball, but Dad and Josh liked to listen on summer nights while we ate dinner, with the lights off if it was a clear evening. If I were at school right now, I would probably be eating with my new roommate, or in some forced group out at some picnic or something. I wouldn't be listening to baseball, or the neighbors' kids playing, or the motorboats on the lake, or the mechanical sounds of the cicadas. The lightning bugs began to blink in the yard and the flagstones on the kitchen floor cooled as we ate hamburgers Josh had grilled out on the brick patio. Superhero lay under the table with his head on top of my bare feet. The night was lovely, but I felt like my being there was ruining it a little bit.

Dad asked Josh about heading to school, if he had gas in the tank, if he was all packed up, what his friends had done over the summer. I watched them talk. Neither looked in my direction. Germaine stared at me, so I looked back and blinked, hard, sort of like *I Dream of Jeannie*; maybe I could make her disappear. But she just kept staring, her narrow eyes a mixture of boredom and hostility. She looked kind of funny, giving me such a mean look while sitting in front of the happy, flowered lilac-and-green wallpaper, and when I started to smile, she rolled her eyes. *Nice.* She was in a snit because Dad had snapped at her earlier about her failure to volunteer to take on more household duties when she was home. Earlier I had made a point of offering to set the table, which Dad declined.

After dinner, Josh helped me carry up the boxes, which I opened with a little paring knife from the kitchen. I finally felt a little regret. It seemed like such a waste of energy, all that packing and taping and carrying from the weeks before. We'd gone to an office supply store and bought boxes in three different sizes, shiny brown packing tape, and a roll of bubble wrap. There was much fun to be had with packing supplies: I had tried to get Superhero to walk across a sheet of the bubble wrap (to no avail) and liked repeatedly solving the puzzle of turning the flat pieces of cardboard into actual boxes with just a little bending and folding. I didn't want to admit how much pleasure I had gotten out of perfectly filling those boxes and sealing them shut neatly with a big plastic tape dispenser. I had spent weeks packing, first the new stuff that I wouldn't need until I got to Kenyon, then slowly the things from home that I wanted to take with me. It made me sad to watch my room get barer and barer as posters, pictures, and favorite books all went in the boxes.

But it was going to be unpacked all at once.

Unhappily I discovered that despite my precise folding, after the long day of loading and driving and unloading, my clothes were all shifted and wrinkled inside the boxes, which irritated me. I hung most things up and put the stuff that needed ironing in a separate pile on my desk. Putting things away was one of my favorite hobbies.

Dad knocked on the door.

"Cecily?"

"Yes?" Here it was. Here was where I was going to have to explain what the hell was going on. I had better come up with something good, unless I could continue to avoid the whole conversation.

He came in and closed the door behind him. He took off his black-rimmed glasses and wiped them on a corner of his shirt.

"You're unpacking?"

"Yes."

"So . . . I suppose that means you're not thinking we'd try this again tomorrow."

"No, Dad. I just can't do this now."

"And you're completely sure? Because I'm willing to try this again tomorrow, no complaining, no questions asked. Or we can see if there's someone you can talk to at Kenyon, or anywhere else for that matter, if you're having doubts."

I shook my head. "No."

"Is everything okay, Cecily? This is just . . . very surprising."

I knew what he meant. I wasn't a dramatic gesture kind of girl. I just wished I could explain what had happened, or say that I knew what would happen next. I still really couldn't believe that I had done it. "Yeah, Dad. I need to figure some stuff out, I guess. I don't know what yet."

He glanced around my room, and his eyes landed on a

**an off year**

little wooden toy chest I kept in the corner to house a few old stuffed bears and rabbits from childhood that I never took out anymore but couldn't bring myself to get rid of. "I suppose . . . I guess . . . I don't see how it could hurt to have you stick around here for a bit longer. If you're really not ready yet."

"Yes. That's what I want. Lucky you, right?"

"Yeah, right. Although . . ." He hesitated. "I won't lie. It won't be bad having you here at home for a little while longer."

"Especially since Josh is leaving and Germaine sucks so bad. I'm the only fun one."

He smiled, but he rubbed the corners of his eyes with his index fingers. He was trying to be nice but was exhausted.

"I'm sorry I made you drive all that way for nothing."

"There's more to it than that," he said. "We have to talk to the people at Kenyon. We have tuition money to deal with. We need to figure out what exactly is coming next."

Suddenly that gut-sick feeling that had been absent all day came to me: I wasn't sure if it was the realization of what I had done, or what I had almost done. My life would already be completely different if I were back in Ohio. But I couldn't deal with that at that moment. I needed to act like I knew what I was doing.

"Of course," I said, "but not tonight. Is that okay?"

He nodded, sighed, turned around, and closed the door behind him, leaving me with the boxes I still had to empty and fold up.


When I woke up the next morning, everything felt the same as before I left. I could hear lifeguard whistles coming from the beach. My comforter smelled like clean. Superhero stuck his nose in my face. Only it was all totally different. It was like taking a sick day from school and realizing what happens at home during the day—nothing.

I listened for the telltale signs of Dad leaving for work: the radio getting shut off, the dishwasher door slamming, the old lock turning. I went downstairs in boxer shorts and a T-shirt and ate cereal and read the paper. At that particular moment, I felt kind of smug. I wasn't doing anything—no camp, no job, no homework, no packing for college, no unpacking *at* college. I knew, though, that the remorse would come soon, and then I'd soon have to justify my existence. I wondered if Mom's advice was right: should I do something amazing with my time? I had nothing amazing planned. Unless maybe I had already done it: turning around and leaving college. Now I had who knows how long—maybe all year—to think about why and figure out what to do.

I'd never not had a plan for myself. Or made for me.

**an off year**

# september

**I could only avoid my best friend,** Kate, for about a week before I let her in on the big news. I felt horrible not talking to her—the only times we hadn't spoken daily in high school were when one of us was traveling—but I was just embarrassed. She was off at college doing whatever it is you're supposed to do. I . . . wasn't. I missed her, was dying for someone to talk to about what I had done, and felt ashamed of avoiding her. I tried to pretend that we both needed the week to get settled. She had been e-mailing me since she got to school, but I'd just respond with a noncommittal "ha!" and smiley faces. Finally, one gorgeous day when everyone was out of the house and I couldn't stand how bored I was, I called her.

The funny thing was that Kate and I had a running gag prior to her leaving for school where neither of us was actually going to college. We kept pretending that we were just leaving for summer camp and that we'd be back at high school in the fall. We called it Double-Secret Senior Year.

"Have a good time," I said earlier that summer, lounging on the green velvet chaise in her gigantic bedroom as she packed up her clothes in boxes. "Make sure to bring your swimsuit and your bug spray."

"I'll make you lots of bead bracelets," she said.

I didn't know if she'd think that the fact that I actually did not go to school would be funny-ha-ha or funny-strange. I was terrified of the latter, of her discovering that all along she was too cool to be friends with me. I worried about her coming home and looking at me and laughing, realizing what a baby I was. But I had to talk to someone. It felt like I didn't exist, almost—my dad, Josh, all my friends were taking part in that transition from summer to school year, but I was just *there*. I needed to talk to Kate, to feel better, to hear what life was like in the outside world, even if I didn't want to know.

"WELL, HELLO THERE!" she screamed into the phone when I called. I smiled.

"Hello yourself."

"How are you?"

"Fine, you?"

"Cecily, it's so weird here. I feel like I'm living on Planet College. Like, it's funny, it's just like what you'd think, but WEIRDER."

"Oh yeah?"

"Yeah, do they have you singing the school song all the time?"

"No," I said. I mean, it was true.

"What is up with that? Do they think this is 1927 or something and everyone's going to the games in their raccoon coats?" Kate briefly had an obsession with the Roaring Twenties a few years ago.

"Ha," I said.

"Anyway," she said, "I gotta go. My roommate and I are going to go get dinner while it's early so we won't have to deal with the crowded cafeteria. See you around, clown."

Okay, so I didn't get to tell her right away, but I knew I would have to. I did not want to be part of some wacky movie where I had to pretend I was in college while I wasn't. That seemed exhausting.

Kate was off on the West Coast at a school for people who are smart enough to get into an Ivy League college but are too cool to actually go. She was an only child and a genius. Her parents, both lawyers, were also incredibly rich. Kate herself had two cars: a little white sports car for the warmer weather and a gigantic SUV for wintertime (which she enjoyed driving through empty parking lots late at night after a heavy snowfall to make fresh tracks).

I sat next to Kate in freshman English, and on the very first day of class I decided that she was the most wonderful person I had ever met. I'm not sure what specifically it was that had indicated this to me. Maybe it was that she was wearing army green Converse All Stars that she'd decorated with Wite-Out while all the other girls were wearing new, sparkly flip-flops. Or that when the cutest guy in class said hi to her, she gave him a look like he was a fresh gob of spit on the sidewalk. Or maybe it was when Kaci Kamp whined because we had to read the first chapter of *To Kill a Mockingbird* for class the next day (one of my favorite books) and Kate passed me a note that said, simply, "She sux," before we'd even spoken to each other. I was on her like a lamprey on a shark.

Kate spent her weekends TP-ing houses of the many boys who adored her, walking around town adopting fake accents and talking to strangers, and organizing trips to go bowling or play miniature golf or trek out to the one remaining drive-in movie theater in the county, all while cracking jokes, inventing nonsense sayings, and performing odd dances. She was tall and pale, with a muscular build from years of swimming and sailing the little Sunfish she'd received for her thirteenth birthday. She had long, wavy auburn hair and was totally unself-conscious about her body, throwing herself around and gesticulating wildly as if nobody else in the world were watching. She even created her own dictionary, and at times I forgot if the actual word for the stuff you eat was *food* or *shebooley*. I wished I were as confident (and pretty and rich and smart) as she was.

With no brothers or sisters, Kate enjoyed coming over and "studying" my family, pretending to interview Germaine (to her annoyance) and following Dad around the house. He adored her, and they had a running gag that he was paying her to be my friend. That didn't seem like such a bad idea, now.

The day after our phone conversation, I called Kate back and told her the truth. "Okay, so I had something else to tell you that I didn't get to. I'm not at Kenyon. I got to school and turned around and went home, and I've been here ever since. I didn't want to tell you."

"I wish I had done that," she said, after a second. "That is so awesome."

I smiled. "It doesn't feel very awesome," I said. "Yet."

"Well, you'll make it awesome," she said. "Why'd you do it, anyway?"

"That's the thing. I don't know," I said. "It's not *like* me, my dad said."

"Well, this is the new you," she said. I liked the idea of a "new" me, but I thought that always entailed a new, empowering attitude, not to mention a new hairstyle. I had neither.

"I made an appointment for you next week with Dr. Stern. She sounds nice," said Dad as he folded one of the navy towels, fresh from the dryer, from Josh's and my bathroom. I suppose that I could have done it myself, since the towels wouldn't even be in use if I weren't at home, but I didn't want to interrupt him.

"Cecily, are you listening to me?"

"Of course, dear Dad," I said in a robot's voice, but really as I stood with my chin in my hands, feeling the vibrations of the washing machine through my elbows, I was staring at the intense orange of the Tide with Bleach box, which somehow reminded me of the Chip 'n' Dale cartoon I had watched earlier that morning. I knew that it involved throwing apple cores at Donald Duck, but what was the *theme*?

My father draped a sheet of lint over my head. I gagged and staggered around the laundry room.

"Pay attention."

"Oh yeah, well, it's all fun and games until somebody chokes on sweater fuzz."

"You know I love you. Almost as much as I love Josh and Germaine. But you have to get out of the house and at least address what happened. Please? It's been almost a month, Cecily, and it doesn't seem like you've done much more than rot your brain in front of the TV. That can't be very helpful. Plus, it was hard to get an appointment with this woman."

I went back to the Tide box. *Man, that's orange.*

He continued. "I think Health and Human Services will come and take you away if we don't at least try to figure out what went wrong. You just need to meet with her once, I promise. Nothing too intense. They're not going to give you a lobotomy. I'll just take care of that myself. I just need to find an ice pick."

"How about I just lie on the couch and talk to you? That'll be much cheaper."

Dad sighed. I took that as my cue to make a grand exit and tore up the stairs from the basement to the kitchen.

Germaine stood crying in front of the toaster.

"Hey, Germy, why are you crying? What did the toaster ever do to you?"

She turned around, tweezers in her hand. "The natural light's better in here than in my bathroom." She dabbed at her eyes with a paper towel and experimentally raised and lowered her newly defined arches. I had to admit, she did a good job—if she was aiming to look like an evil villain. She looked critically at my brows. "You know, you could use a tweezing. You've got good definition, you just need a cleanup."

My hands flew protectively to my brows. "Don't you come near me with those things! The last time you tried to make me over, you sent me to the emergency room!"

"It wasn't my fault you poked yourself in the eye when you were goofing around with my eyeliner." I couldn't really dispute this. I was ten and wanted to look like Cleopatra but instead came home from the hospital with an eye patch, looking like a pirate.

I pulled two slices of cinnamon raisin bread from the bag on the counter. My sister watched me as I painstakingly picked out the raisins and flicked them into the sink.

"Why do you have Dad buy that bread if you don't like raisins?"

"I don't like the raisins themselves, but their essence is important in the toast."

"Well, don't make a mess, please. Conrad is coming over soon."

Conrad. The name filled me with intense feelings of blandness. I always hated Germaine's boyfriends, and the funny thing is, I don't think that she was too fond of them herself. She was looking for a knight in a power suit, but this one, like the others, was a rickety sideburned hipster in stale-smelling vintage shirts. He called himself a writer, which meant nothing in particular but an annoying tendency to try to be deep. However, in mannerisms and conversation, he was so unsure of himself that I felt like I could push him over at any time with my finger. And Conrad was a terrible writer. The odes he wrote about their lukewarm relationship tended to be bizarrely pornographic. Germaine kept them stashed in her makeup bag in her bathroom.

"All right," I said, but realized that without thinking I was already squashing the raisins in the sink with my thumb, fat and flat like dead black flies. Superhero was crammed between my knees and the sink, his head down, intently watching the floor for falling treats.

**september**

"Cecily, can you take Superhero for a walk? Conrad's a little . . . uh . . ."

"Impotent? Gay? Smelly?"

Germaine glared. "He doesn't like dogs."

"Then why is he going out with you?" I said. Before she could snap back at me, I dodged out the door with Superhero, onto the driveway, and down the street toward the beach.

It had just rained, so the effect of the sunshine on the lake mixed with the dark clouds moving east painted the water a silvery iridescent color. The leaves glowed gold, and the slick blacktop on the street shined.

One time a few years ago when I was walking Superhero on a foggy spring day, the lake was a milky jade green, unlike anything I had ever seen before. It was maybe forty degrees out, but I still wanted to jump in. The sad thing about Lake Michigan photo-op moments is that the water always looks so inviting, but when you walk up to it, it's still the same grayish brown it always is. You expect the lake to look as magical as it did from afar, but it is always a letdown.

Dad grew up in San Francisco and was used to looking at water, so when he and my mom moved to Chicago's North Shore after they got married, they bought a house across the street from Lake Michigan. In the summer, sandy, bawling rug rats in diapers and idiotic flat-voiced girls working on their tans dominate the beach, but in the colder seasons, it's a nice place to wander around without being scrutinized by the high school lifeguards. Unfortunately, no matter the season, the beauty of the lake still guaranteed a healthy risk of running into people I knew from the neighborhood.

I escaped Germaine and her tweezers only to run straight

on into Mrs. Garfield, my middle school algebra teacher, who happened to live down the street. She was also the mother of my former friend Meg. Meg and I used to be inseparable, and then suddenly we weren't for various reasons including her being a massive bitch. We hadn't really talked since junior year, which was going to make seeing her mom nice and awkward. The thought of Meg knowing that I wasn't at school was mortifying.

"Hello, Cecily," Mrs. Garfield said, looking startled to see me.

"Hi, Mrs. Garfield." Just steps from the sand, Superhero tried his hardest to yank my arm out of its socket.

She looked at me closely, like I was a math problem she was writing on the projection screen. "How are you doing? How is school going?"

"School is fine!" I said. "It's great." I was sure that it was, somewhere, for somebody.

"You're home on a break?"

"Yes," I said, hoping she would keep asking me questions that were so easy to lie about, which was much simpler than having to explain what I was really up to. I imagined her going home and talking about me matter-of-factly with her family over their dinner. *Cecily didn't go to school. I wonder what happened. You know, I'm really not surprised. Pass the pork tenderloin, please.* I really hoped she wouldn't tell Meg that she saw me.

Mrs. Garfield nodded. We stood still, looking at each other. This was like the verbal equivalent of the staring game: I wasn't going to say anything. She remained silent.

"Yes, well," she finally said, making me the winner. "You take care of yourself, now. Tell your father I said hello."

"Will do." I speed-walked to the beach to get the awkwardness of the conversation behind me.

When we hit the beach, I let Supes off the leash, and all seventy-five hairy pounds of him were off, running through the shallow waves and sticking his black nose in the sand. I picked my way along the waterfront, pocketing stones and shouting to Superhero. Only two other people were out there, a father and his toddler. We passed each other, and I gave the father an adult-serious nod-smile but stuck my tongue out at the kid. He hid behind his dad's knees.

I thought I was pretty good at high school. You go to this class, you go to that class, you do this activity and that one, you make nice with your friends and your teachers, and you do some homework. Although I did hate shuffling around doing the same thing every day with the same people. By the time graduation came around, I was done with most of them, ready to get away from them—I would keep in touch with my good friends, I figured, but I wasn't going to go around on my last day of school making sure everybody signed my yearbook, as if I were always going to be BFF with Vanessa from that one English class or Darnell from sophomore-year second-semester gym.

I wasn't the prom queen, but I wasn't the girl from *Carrie*, either. Basically, I had been under the impression that I was pretty functional—I had my good times and some good friends and was sick enough of it to be ready to move to the next phase. After doing pretty well on standardized tests (I liked the order of the tests, except for the essay questions, which tended to be 100 percent bullshit when I wrote them), filling out all those applications, and smiling sincerely in the interviews, I thought I was ready for college.

Maybe talking to somebody about all this wasn't a bad idea. I just felt self-conscious—I didn't feel *crazy*, but I was worried that this so-called doctor would inform me that I had a mental defect or worse—that I was just a big baby who couldn't deal with reality. I still had a feeling that something was brewing with Dad, some big talk or punishment. Unless he was just going to let me get away with it without saying something, like the time he didn't say a word after the mailman slipped and sprained his ankle on the ice that I was supposed to have salted in front of the house. Fortunately, the mailman didn't threaten to sue. I wasn't sure if Kenyon was still asking for its tuition money. Dad hadn't mentioned it again so far. I tried not to think about it. I started feeling guilty. I wondered if Dad was worried that he and Mom had accidentally broken me during their divorce and that the damage was just starting to show now. A little therapy could get me all fixed up.

"Fine, I'll go see the stupid shrink," I said, finding Dad at his desk in his office off the kitchen when I got home from the beach. I never understood how the whole house was usually spotless, but piles of papers were eternally stacked four feet high in his office. Or how he still never seemed to misplace anything.

"Good," he said. "Eleven o'clock on Thursday. I hope you can pry yourself out of bed that early."

"What's this?" asked Germaine, as she and Conrad passed by on their way to the living room.

"Cecily has a doctor's appointment," Dad said, glancing at Conrad.

"A headshrinker!" I said. No need to hide the fact. I was a little excited. I felt kind of special.

"Why don't you just *tell* Cecily to go to school and save some money?" said Germaine. She pointed at me. "Go to school!"

I rolled my eyes.

"Maybe I need to see a shrink, too, to help me find out what kind of job I want," said Germaine. She was just jealous.

"I think all you need to see are the want ads," said Dad.

"Ha-ha," I said to Germaine. She punched me on the arm. Superhero got overexcited and jumped around, almost knocking Germaine over. I felt it was fair.

# october

**I was starting to look forward** to seeing the therapist. Kate was busy with classes and, oh, I don't know, her life, so she couldn't talk all that frequently. I was feeling kind of lonely.

There actually was someone else whom I had been avoiding other than Kate, and it was Mike. Thinking about how I wasn't talking to him only made me feel worse than if I had no one else at all.

I had known Mike since preschool. We spent almost all our free time together when we were kids. Mike was kind of quiet, my listener as I babbled. We'd go to the movies and then out to the only greasy spoon in town for french fries as I jabbered away about whom I would have cast in the movie if I had directed it (usually myself). I'd coax him into making silly home movies with me, or he'd write songs on the piano and I'd make up lyrics about the people who went to our high school.

Then, around junior year, something happened to Mike. Maybe it was when Danielle Hoffmeyer, a senior with a mile of white-blond hair, asked him to prom. Maybe it was when his neck suddenly got thicker. Maybe it was when he let his black hair grow out and suddenly his pale green eyes became a lot more noticeable. Most likely it was just the age when girls start realizing that nice boys like him can be fun to date. Suddenly he became a hot commodity.

I had never really thought about Mike as a dateable person, but a lot of girls started to look at me as either competition or a bailiff they had to bribe to get to him. I got invited to a few pool parties and weekends at summer houses in hopes that I'd bring Mike and then settle quietly into the background while Mike was feted. I quit going after a while: I enjoyed myself when it was just the two of us but became incredibly self-conscious when we hung out with other people. And, while he used to be a music nerd, he somehow suddenly became a music god. When he played his guitar, girls clustered around him, hoping that he'd write a song about them. He wrote one for me called "Cecily, Why You So Silly?" but I was the only one who ever heard it, that I knew of. I kept a copy of the file saved with my special e-mails to listen to if I ever needed it.

I always knew Mike was smart, but I was vaguely surprised and nauseated when I found out he'd gotten into Harvard. The last time I spoke to him was the day he left, heading up early to try out for the crew team. I already felt like we'd been growing apart, and this, going to go participate in a weird East Coast sport up at a famous school, felt like he might as well have been going away to Mars. Since he was still a good guy, Mike didn't leave without saying good-bye—he came over and gave me a stiff hug. He was on his way back from Wendy Maloney's house. She had claimed him as her boyfriend, and he had to comfort her before their departure—as if she had a hope in hell that they'd stay together when she was at the University of Kansas.

"What are you going to do when you don't make the team?" I asked while we stood awkwardly in the driveway, smashed acorn bits from one of our trees poking my bare feet. "You'll never be able to row with those tiny little arms." He flexed one of his not-really-tiny arms like he was on the cover of a bodybuilding magazine and grimaced.

"I guess I'll cry first," he said. "And then I'll just take the extra time to move in. What are you going to do before you head out?"

I shrugged. "Kate and I were thinking about going up to the House on the Rock." It was a crazy tourist attraction in Wisconsin, full of strange collections that a Midwestern eccentric had amassed. Carousels, old nautical equipment, hundreds of thimbles and player pianos. It was going to be awesome.

"I went there once. That place is insanity. You'll love it." I smiled. "Well, I better shove off," he said. "My mom's being really weepy, so I'd better get home so she can talk some more about how I'm all grown up. Good luck with school, Cecily."

"Thanks, good luck at . . . where are you going again?"

He laughed and punched me in the arm. Both of my good friends were smart. I was on the smarter end of average, or maybe the more average end of smart. I took pains not to hang out too often with the two of them at the same time, because I suspected that if they realized how smart they both were—and how dumb I actually was—they would completely cut me out and I'd have to find more mediocre friends for myself. Also, the last time I had introduced Mike to one of my girlfriends, it had ended in disaster.

"Keep in touch," I said.

"I will. You, too."

He gave me a weird, awkward kiss on the cheek and then turned away. And he got into his little brown Volkswagen, backed out, and drove off.

The idea of calling Mike and dorkily saying hi, explaining that I wasn't in school and why, made me physically uncomfortable. We never really had deep talks, anyway. We just goofed around together. I'd call him someday. When I knew what to say for myself.

A week or so after he first mentioned me seeing a therapist, Dad dropped me off in front of the Rotary building, a sad little suburban office building that probably really wanted to be a grown-up office building like the ones in Chicago but instead found itself housing mostly two-bit dentists. It smelled like rubber, antiseptic, static electricity, and office supplies. The security guard didn't even bother to look up as my turquoise Pumas squeaked through the black marbled lobby. I looked up Dr. Stern's name on the backlit directory board and took the elevator to the third floor.

On the third floor, I walked past the doors of several doctors' offices with old-fashioned gold writing on the frosted glass doors. On my door was printed MEDICAL OFFICES. That didn't seem very promising.

The waiting room was lit with warm, soothing lamps, probably to prevent any fluorescent-light-related freakouts. A pretty Hispanic girl, maybe a few years older than Germaine, sat behind the desk, ignoring me. A nameplate stood on her desk: GINA, surrounded by pink Valentine heart stickers.

"Hi," I said. She raised her eyes but didn't say anything. She looked annoyed. In fact, she looked just like Germaine did when I walked into the living room when she and Conrad were watching a movie: not happy to see me.

"Um, I'm here to see Dr. Stern."

Still the look.

"I'm Cecily Powell?" Maybe a name would spring her into action.

"She'll be with you in a few minutes," she said, sighing. "Have a seat."

"Thanks, thanks a lot," I said. We were off to a good start.

*"You're welcome,"* she snapped back. If Dr. Stern was as much fun as her receptionist, this was going to be interesting.

All the magazines in the waiting room were terrible. They catered only to rich people, old people, or women with babies. I picked up a *New Yorker* and started flipping through, looking at the cartoons, which were boring, too.

I kept an eye on the receptionist to see if she was shooting me some sort of hex, but she kept her head down in her paperwork.

I didn't have any idea of what Dr. Stern would look like, other than a vague memory of the woman who sometimes played a shrink on *Law & Order*, which I liked to watch when I was sick. But a woman barely older than the receptionist came out into the lobby.

"Cecily?" she said. "Hi, come on in, I'm Jane Stern." She shook my hand quickly and then scurried off down the hall, leaving me to practically run after her. She was a tiny woman (shorter than me, which is pretty shrimpy) but was powering along on her little legs in four-inch dark green alligator heels beneath a belted khaki-colored dress. She wore her hair in a layered, highlighted brown bob and looked like she should have been working in a high-end department store, not a doctor's office. She waved me into a room that felt more like a bathroom than an office. The floor was linoleum, and plastic cabinets and counters lined the wall. We sat down in two desk chairs, the kind that spin around and have seats that you can raise and lower.

"Isn't it awful in here?" she said, apparently reading my mind. "This used to be a medical doctor's office back in the day, and they haven't put in carpeting or anything yet. Anyway, so tell me why you're here."

Jane Stern still didn't strike me as being BFF material, but to be honest, I hadn't really talked to anyone in a while other than Dad or Germaine. So I was kind of in a chatty mood. I told her about what had happened.

I told her what I thought about high school—how I graduated and then spent a long, lazy summer (which went by too quickly) going to the pool and driving around with friends, going to the city and sitting in the backyard with Dad, trying to make sure each hamburger we barbecued, each lemonade we drank outside was perfect, because who knew what life would be like the next time I came home. I could become like Josh or Germaine, not wanting to hang out with him, and that would be sad.

I told her how the summer was tainted with these thoughts and the stress of getting ready for school, thinking about school, thinking about what stuff I needed to get and what my roommate would be like and how my classes would be. It started to seem so bizarre to me—this huge life change that most everybody I knew was going to go through—and we all had to do it. But as soon as those kind of thoughts crept into my head, it was time to go to Target and Bed Bath & Beyond to buy a shower caddy, pillows, and a blanket, just like you're supposed to. It was just so completely, abruptly different from the last eight years, but none of us questioned it. I e-mailed with my future roommate, Molly, so we could check each other out. She seemed decent enough. I felt mostly ready. I thought.

Then it was time. Dad and I loaded up the car, left at an ungodly hour, and made a mostly quiet six-hour drive to Ohio. And then, just like that, it was time to go back.

"So here I am now."

"And what did your dad do when you told him you weren't staying?"

I shrugged. "Nothing. He asked if I was sure. Then he asked where I wanted to have lunch."

"Was that it?"

"Pretty much."

"Is that a typical response from your father?"

"What do you mean?"

"Somebody else's father might have rejected your decision."

"Or they'd just go ahead and kick their kid's butt."

She smiled. "That, too."

"I've never really thought about it. But Dad's always pretty much let me do what I want."

"Is that so?"

"Yeah, but that's just how we get along. I guess I maybe should have expected more of a reaction from Dad, like, I don't know, yelling or something. But we didn't talk about it on the way home, or when we got home, or anything. We've talked about it a little bit since then, but not much."

"Have you talked to any of your friends from high school since you've been back?"

"A little."

"Did you have a lot of friends in high school?"

"Not, like, a ton. A few close friends." She made a note, and I examined the floor beneath my feet like there was going to be a test on it later.

"So why do you think you ended up not going to school?"

"I don't know." I said. "I just got there and it didn't feel right. Like, I had just gone with the flow with the whole application process and didn't really think about what I was doing, and I got there and was just like, *Holy shit—wait a second.* I freaked."

"Have you ever had problems leaving home before? Home-sickness?"

"No. Not really. I mean, I never loved traveling with my mom that much, but that was mostly because it sucked, not because I was homesick."

"Ah."

We talked for a while more, about what I expected to happen in college, about Dad, about Mom, about Josh and Germaine. I felt the gist of what she was writing down was that I was a big baby and I was completely spoiled by Dad. Fortunately, for a therapist, there are only fifty minutes in an hour, and we were done quickly.

"Well, Cecily," Dr. Stern said at the end, "I think it's a good idea to go ahead and take your year off. Relax, enjoy the time you have with your family—you might just get sufficiently sick of them so that you'll just want to go back. However, I'm still not totally clear on why you're here right now, and I don't think you are, either. I'm thinking that it's a mild anxiety issue, but it's hard to know after just one visit. I'd like you to come back next month."

Damn. I was hoping that miraculously she could tell me what was wrong with me and perhaps give me some sort of pill to fix it, all in one visit.

Gina was examining her split ends when I got back to reception. "Hey. Do I need to, like, do anything to check out?" I asked. "Or am I set to go?" She looked up without raising her head and cracked her gum loudly. She sighed and turned three inches to the left, picking up a business card using her long, silver-painted nails as if they were tweezers.

"Oh no, thanks," I said.

"It's your appointment card," she said. "For next time."

"It's okay, I'll remember the date. Thanks."

"TAKE IT," she said in a voice that was nearly a shout.

"Jesus Christ, okay," I said. Gina shot me a very evil look, but then fortunately her phone rang and it was time to escape.

The frosted glass door closed behind me, and the rest of the day stretched ahead. So. I officially had a year to fix whatever was currently wrong with me. That seemed easy. I just had to figure out what it was that I needed to fix.

I walked home, kicking up little bunches of dried leaves on the sidewalk where they'd begun to fall, saying under my breath, "I'm taking the year off," to practice it. In case I ran into Mrs. Garfield again, in case I had to explain it on a job application or something, in case I just needed to convince myself.

"I'm taking time off." That sounded good. I had heard people use that phrase before. It sounded nice, relaxing, practically professional. I was taking time off from school—to do something. I just wasn't sure *what*. If anybody asked, I would just say that it was personal. I was going on sabbatical. My dad's colleagues did that sometimes. That seemed very serious and somehow almost religious to me. But those people seemed to be actually doing something with their time. I was pretty sure they were working on a book or some project, not sitting at home in their slippers watching *All My Children*.

"So?" said Dad later that day when he got home from work.

"It was fine," I said. "It was whatever."

"Can you use some more specific words, please?"

"She thinks it's a good idea for me to take the year off. You know, to relax."

"Just relax? I didn't know that you were stressed out to begin with."

I shrugged my shoulders.

"Did she say if I need to come in? Did she say what she thought the problem was?" he asked.

"No, you don't. And she said that maybe it's anxiety."

"Anxiety?"

"Yeah, anxiety. Why?"

He just shook his head and muttered, "The women in this family . . ."

"The women in this family what?" I'd never heard myself lumped together with my mom and sister. If Dad complained about us, it was usually because Germaine and I were fighting, or I didn't want to go visit Mom, or Mom and Germaine were both pains in the ass. But never all three of us together.

"Nothing," he said.

"What?" I asked again. I knew there was something mean coming, but it felt like it was time for Dad to get mad at me. I wanted him to get mad at me.

"Well, none of you is exactly an overachiever," he snapped. I opened my mouth, but I knew that whatever I was going to say wouldn't make it untrue. What could I do? Demand that he take me seriously for having skipped out on my first year of college? Doing the dishes every now and then didn't really count. This conversation needed to be steered elsewhere before I started feeling too ashamed. I didn't want to be a letdown like Mom and Germaine.

"I'm fun, though, right?" I asked, deciding to play the fun card. That was always a fun card to play.

"You're sometimes fun," he said.

"And at least I'm around," I said.

"Germaine is around," he said.

"But I'm fun," I said, poking him in his black sweater. "I'm fun and around. Germaine is just around but no fun at all.

Josh is sometimes fun, but he's not around. I'm both. Do you see what I'm getting at here? I'm fun and around."

"There is no denying that," he said. "And I actually do like having you around." He gave me a smooch on the cheek, and I wiped it off in pretend disgust and went upstairs before he asked me to do anything. I felt guilty, like I was getting away with something.

# november

**Dad's little comment** about Mom, Germaine, and me was still bugging me by the next time I went to see Jane, which I didn't do entirely willingly. I felt nervous that I didn't have much to tell her, like I was supposed to come up with something to explain myself but I had failed. I kind of hoped I could skip the therapy thing and work my issues out magically on my own.

I intended to lie low until Thanksgiving, emerge to eat, and then hide away again until Christmas, but stupid Gina from Dr. Stern's office had to go calling the house to confirm my appointment. The worst part was that Germaine got the call.

"Dr. Stern's office called to remind you of your appointment tomorrow," she announced one night over dinner.

"Ah. Interesting! Thank you," I said, hoping to avoid drawing attention to the matter, as I tried unsuccessfully to twirl a neat forkful of spaghetti. I shoved the pasta and its dangling tendrils in my mouth.

"Oh yeah," said Dad. "Do you need a ride? What time is the appointment?"

"It's at two," said Germaine. I shot her the death stare.

"I don't think I really need to go," I said. "I'm fine. Really!"

"Really!" said Dad. "What have you done for the last two months?"

"I've been helping out around the house," I said. This was true. I had organized our DVDs alphabetically, cleaned out the closets (except Germaine's, which I wasn't allowed near), and untangled all the knots of electrical cord in the house. And yet somehow that didn't satisfy Dad.

"Cecily, it's probably a good idea for you to go," said Germaine. "What's the worst that can happen?"

"You stay out of this," I said. "You haven't been doing shit, either."

"Okay," said Dad, raising his voice just enough. "Germaine, you shut up. Cecily, you're going. No complaining."

Germaine and I rolled our eyes in unison and then glared at each other suspiciously.


"Hey, Gina," I said as I entered Dr. Stern's office the next day. I was curious to see if maybe she was a decent human being and we'd get along better this time—maybe she was just having a bad day last time. However, instead of returning my hello, she immediately picked up the phone to make a call. But before I could plan my next move, the door opened, and within a few minutes I was telling Jane what my dad said about "the women in this family."

"What did he mean by that?" She was wearing a little cape, which seemed very expensive and would probably look ridiculous on me, but was perfect on her.

"Well," I said. "We have kinda all done a bad job making something of ourselves. I blame Mom."

"That's what they all say," said Jane, and I made a face at her and told her about my mother.

I don't remember too much about what it was like when Mom lived with us, except that she wasn't around a lot. I mostly remember that she left Dad the summer we trapped raccoons.

It was a very exciting summer for me, at first. It turned out that the previous winter, raccoons ripped up the shingles on our roof to try to get inside for warmth. Horrified, Mom called exterminators, but she was told that with this particular kind of raccoon problem, there was only one thing that could be done.

We procured a raccoon-size trap from Animal Control, which was to be baited nightly after we set it up on the side of the house near the tree the raccoons used to clamber onto the roof. The trap, which looked like an oversize wire shoe box, would shut its door after the raccoon stepped on a spring-mounted switch on its way to the food. There it would wait, unharmed, at least until morning, when the Animal Control man took it away and, as I understood it, let it loose into a happy, sunny woodland area to rejoin its cute raccoon families.

Germaine surprisingly excelled at trapping the raccoons,

despite being generally grossed out by most animals. Every time Dad set the bait, we'd end up with an empty trap, the neighbor's cat, or a possum, which the Animal Control man would haul out of the trap and carry by the tail, splay-limbed and stoic, and throw in the back of the truck for relocation. Germaine really had a knack for baiting the raccoons, though. She checked online to see what foods raccoons liked and added the ingredients to the grocery list. Every night she would carefully bait the trap with corn on the cob, fruit, tuna, and peanut butter, varying the meals and scattering them throughout the trap. It was really quite artful. She would step out after dinner armed with a flashlight, ignoring the mosquitoes that were excited by her minimal tank top, and carefully place each piece of food as if she were setting a table for some important diplomat. Every time Germaine set the trap, we trapped a fat, angry raccoon that would try to dig its way out. It could have been a career for her.

The traps were laid on the side of the house, directly under my bedroom willow. If I stayed awake late enough, I'd inevitably hear the snap of the trap as a raccoon stumbled into it, another victory for Germy. Sometimes I'd hear the raccoon crying, a ghostly noise that sounded like a loon.

One morning I woke up to pouring rain. I knew that the trap had caught its prey from the familiar snap and the crying that had gone on all night. It was only 6:30 A.M., though, and I realized the animal must have been sitting in the rain for hours, with hours still to go before the Animal Control truck arrived. Although I felt so comfy in my bed and had just woken up from a great dream where we had beds in school instead of desks, I decided to do something for the poor creature. I ran down to the kitchen, congratulating myself on my selflessness, pulled out a large garbage bag, and cut apart the seams. Throwing on Dad's raincoat, I ran outside and faced the raccoon. It did not look any different from the other raccoons, but I liked to think it held an expression of misery, combined with gratitude at my presence, as it hunched over, sopping wet. I draped the bag over the cage, providing a shelter from the rain, and ran back inside, upstairs, and into bed, feeling like I had done a good deed.

I woke up around 10:00 A.M., after the rain had stopped, and found my family downstairs at the breakfast table, with the exception of Mom, who had gone out to play tennis.

"Did the Animal Control man come yet?" I asked.

"Yeah," Josh said. Nobody looked at me.

I frowned. I had expected at least one of them, especially Dad or Josh, to say something about my kindness. "Did you notice anything about the cage?"

"Yeah, actually, there was a garbage bag inside the cage," said Germaine.

"It was inside the cage?" The spaces between the mesh were barely large enough to stick the tip of your finger between, were you so brave.

"Yes," she said testily. "What were you doing?"

"I put a garbage bag over the cage."

"Oh," said Germy, pretending to read the classifieds section. "I guess he pulled it inside. Why did you do that?"

"Because he had to sit out there in the rain," I cried. "Even if he's in a cage, he didn't have to get soaked."

Dad patted me on the head. "Our Lady of Mercy," he chuckled.

"Yeah, right," said Germaine. "More like Our Lady of Uselessness."

"Our Lady of the Slightly Less Uncomfortable Fate," added Josh.

"What are you talking about?"

"You don't know?" asked Josh.

"What?"

"Oh!" said Germaine, clearly relishing this. "They kill the raccoons after we catch them. We thought you knew."

That day didn't feel that much different from when I learned about Santa Claus and the Tooth Fairy and the not-existing.

Dad must have told Mom about it, because when she came home she handed me a Blow Pop and could barely suppress one of those infuriating "Oh, this kid is so angry but it's really pretty funny" smirks. I felt like a baby. I hated it. I hated being treated like a baby.

That was the last memory I had of my mom, good or bad, living at home with us. And then, one day a few weeks later, she just went out in the morning and never came home. We had heard nothing of a luncheon with her girlfriends, a doctor's appointment, a tennis lesson, anything. Well, we kids hadn't, anyway. The phone rang around dinnertime, and Dad answered it. He called us all downstairs to the kitchen to tell us that Mom would be away for a little while, to figure things out. I didn't see her go or even notice that her stuff was gone. She would take care of that a few weeks later while Dad took us on a trip to visit Mom's parents (an excruciating stay, in that normally-quiet-but-kind Grandma and Grampa treated us like we were preemies, whispering around us and stroking our heads). By that point, we knew what was going on and it was no surprise.

"Are you guys getting a divorce?" Germaine had asked bluntly the night that Dad first gathered us together around the kitchen table.

"We'll see," said Dad. "Maybe. I don't know."

They all turned to me as if they expected me to say something, or cry, or yell. But all I could say was, "Is that all?"

"For now, I suppose, yes," said Dad.

"So then I ran upstairs to watch TV," I told Jane.

"That's how you responded?"

"I know," I said. "I felt bad about it later. I was sad, but I knew it was going to happen. Mom and Dad had been arguing, it seemed, my entire life. They didn't even seem to *like* each other. It was just a matter of time. I was sad that Dad was sad, but I knew there was nothing I could do about it."

"Hmm," said Jane. "That makes sense."

"Yeah," I said. "So. It's been just Dad ever since, which is fine because I think even before they got divorced I liked hanging out with him much more. He gets me or something."

"And he likes the idea of you taking a year off?" Jane asked.

"I think so. I think he thinks if I think it's a good idea, then it is."

"And you think it was the right choice?"

I tried to think of what I'd be doing if I were at school that very moment and not sitting with Dr. Stern. An image of high school all over again popped into my head: going to school with, eating with, and worst of all living with people I didn't necessarily like. "I guess . . . how could it be better to be in college and be around all these strangers—and have to blend in with them and get along with them—than to be at home? It might be boring, but I know what's up here. I'm not cool, but nobody's decided I'm uncool." I wasn't sure if I had made this up just to please her or if it was true.

"Have you always worried about being uncool?"

"No," I said. "I mean, not that I know of. Maybe. I don't know." A few uncomfortable flashbacks popped into my head, like finding my one solitary picture in the yearbook, and going to junior prom with Meg, who ended up leaving with a guy, so I had to get home by myself.

"But you think you'll either be cool—or just not care if you're cool—by next year?"

"Maybe," I said. "Yeah, maybe I won't be as stressed about it." Jane was asking tougher questions this time, firing back with more questions. "What about you, do *you* think I'll be ready?"

"Well, I don't know you well enough yet," she said. "Although at first glance I'd say you're probably already more ready than you know. There was a part of me that wanted to tell you to go right back where you came from."

"Why didn't you?"

Jane smiled. "Because I think just choosing not to go is a bigger deal than you think it is. Even if you're choosing not to do something, you're still making a choice. Maybe it's not a bad thing. But it's something worth taking your time to consider—don't just pretend it didn't happen."

"Hmm."

"There's nothing wrong with taking the year off," Jane said. "But I think you need help making the most of it and using it to prep for what lies ahead—even if it's not school."

"Fine," I said. "Sounds good." I resisted the urge to spin around in my chair.

"Cecily, what I typically offer is something called cognitive-behavioral therapy, which basically means that I give you some exercises to try to make this year a good one, to prepare you to take the next steps, and we see how that works. Eventually I want you to get out of the house more, and I also think down the line it might be interesting to see what happens after some planned one-on-one time with your sister."

"That sounds like a nightmare," I said. "Anyway, it's not like we don't spend time together now. Maybe we spend too much time together."

"Well, that might come later. Right now, I'm going to give you an assignment," said Jane. "But you need to be willing to work with me. Do you think you can do that?" I nodded and tried to appear cooperative. I was so bored from the last month, I was willing to take orders from a stranger. And even if I still couldn't figure out why I had turned around in August, maybe it wouldn't matter as long as I'd be able to move forward eventually. "I want you to just get in touch with at least one old friend from high school that you haven't yet. Won't your friends be back soon for Thanksgiving break? It's not healthy for you not to hang out with anybody your age. And maybe it'll help you talk to someone you trust. You'll feel better."

"I'm embarrassed," I said.

"Why?" she asked.

"Because I'm lame and they're in school," I said. I couldn't believe I was saying this. I wish I at least had a more mature way of getting this across. "I mean, I feel like a baby or something."

"So what?" she said. "Do you really think they'll think you're a baby?"

"No," I said. "I guess not."

"And even if they do, what happens then?"

"Um, I guess I won't have any friends then?"

"And then what?"

"And then what *what*? Then I'd be really screwed and really pathetic. And then I'm sure you'd get really rich because I could come and talk to you about that all the time."

Jane laughed. "Okay, take it easy. See your friends—I'm sure they'll be happy to hear from you. I'll see you afterward, and we'll discuss what went down." She wrote on a piece of plain white paper my name, the date, and "Rx: See @ least 1 friend." Her handwriting was unexpectedly cramped and scrawly.

"Is this an official document?" I asked. "Did they not get you a prescription pad yet?"

"I don't write prescriptions," she said. "This is just a reminder for you. Or you can toss it when you leave."

"And what happens next?" I asked.

"We'll see when we meet," she said. "See you later."

I had to admit I liked Jane, despite her giving me assignments. Or maybe because she was giving me assignments. It was hard to believe that we had to pay someone to tell me to look up my friends, but I must have done something to deserve needing a professional to remind me to do it instead of sitting at home waiting for *Simpsons* reruns to come on and petting Superhero. I certainly liked Jane more than I liked Gina, who simply left my reminder card on the reception desk and didn't say anything. I slid the card off the counter and headed out without saying anything to her, either.

Dad was at work when I got home. I went to my room and pinned Jane's "prescription" to my bulletin board, which I had totally cleared off before leaving for college. It felt good to have something up there again. But something was churning in the pit of my stomach, and it was that even though Jane was right about me seeing my friends, I was worried about things with Kate. I had called to complain to her a few times over the past few weeks about how bored I was, and I think she was getting a little sick of me.

"Cecily, it's hot. Everyone here knows someone who decided to take a gap year," Kate had said. "They go build shelters in Africa or promise to write in a journal every day or work on a pot farm or whatever. And then they're supposed to come back like all worldly and whatnot. Hey, I gotta go, we're heading to the gym."

The gym? Since when did Kate go to the gym? When we were in high school, we competed for who could get the slower time on the mile run. I had a feeling she wasn't listening to me anyway. I would have felt better if it were "a gap year" and I had some noble pursuit I was going to follow for a year, something to show for myself, something that I knew would make me a more mature person. But I had no idea what I was going to do, and I wasn't sure if I was maybe becoming less mature by the minute.

As I stared at the bulletin board now, I thought about how calling Mike would go. I didn't want to call him just to sound stupid—I especially didn't want to have him think I had a crush on him or something. This had never worried me before, but now he had a long-distance girlfriend and I was home alone. To get the image out of my head of me stammering on the phone while he and all his college friends (who would be listening in, for some reason) laughed at me, I went into the hall and tossed a tennis ball against Germaine's door until she came out and yelled at me.

I knew Kate would be coming home for Thanksgiving break, and I wanted to see her, just talk to her and feel normal again. After Germaine kicked me out of the hallway, I finally turned on my cell phone (which I had been keeping off lately) and gave Kate a call. I had always assumed that we'd be best friends until we were withered and old and throwing things at young people from our wheelchairs. I worried that the friendship was weakening.

"A-wooga, a-wooga," she said when she picked up the phone. "Where have you been?"

"Literally?"

"Sure."

"At the shrink's."

"Whoa. What was that like?"

"Not as fun as you would think."

"Anybody want a peanut?" Kate said, a line from *The Princess Bride* that we always used when one of us accidentally rhymed. "Anyway, what did he say? Did he send you to an institution? Is he giving you a lobotomy? Are you taking pills? Did you meet a giant Indian who threw a sink out the window?"

"She said I'm taking this year off because I have some issues and maybe I can work them out."

"Issues of what? Magazines? That doesn't seem very fair." I heard a guy yelling in the background and then a muffling sound like she was covering up the phone with her hand. "You better put that away, dickhead, before I call the cops on you! Get out!" Some giggling. Then the muffling sound again. "Sorry," she said. "Neighbor issues. Seriously, are you okay?"

"Yeah, I'm fine," I said, patting Superhero, who had just trotted up. "I guess my biggest problem is that I just don't know why exactly all this went down. If I needed to explore the world, then I could go do that. If I needed to start off at a community college, I could do that. But I don't know what I need yet."

"Well," she said, and her voice changed awkwardly, as it did when she was being serious. "I'm here for you."

"I know," I said. "So what's going on with you?"

"Actually," she said, "I have to get to class. But I'm coming home in a few days and I want to see you. I'll give you a call when I'm in. See you in hell." She hung up, and I smiled at the phone.

I felt so much better that I put on my coat and went out to the movies by myself, something I'd never done before. I was disappointed that Dad was at work, because I was excited to show him how carefree and independent I was, how I was enjoying my time off and not just lying around the house. When I got to the theater, though, I realized I had been so focused on the task at hand that I had forgotten to see what was playing. I ended up seeing some romantic comedy about a woman who loves a man, but he has to go to the moon on a mission. It was pretty awful.

I wasn't sure when, but sometime over the last few years the coffeehouses in town had turned into impromptu day cares. The moms had pushed out even the college kids who came with their white laptops to pretend to study even though they were all looking at porn. When I got to the café where I was going to meet Kate, I had to pick my way around toys scattered on the floor and ignore a three-year-old who accidentally tugged on my peacoat and called me "Mommy" as I ordered, before he realized his error and ran off. It was a miracle that I found an open couch that wasn't being used for story time or changing diapers.

I plopped down and started to read an *Us Weekly* magazine I had splurged on. I loved being told how celebrities were just like me. Apparently they leaned on fences, drank coffee, even obeyed the laws of gravity, just like little old me!

"Excuse me, but do you mind if I breast-feed here?" I looked up.

There was Kate. She looked the same, yet different. It took me a second to figure out what it was. She was wearing some makeup, and her clothes were hugging her body a little bit more than they used to. She was wearing a short white puffy parka instead of her old olive wool military topcoat.

"Only if I can watch." I stood up and gave her a hug, and she almost squeezed the life out of me. I'd forgotten how good and tight her hugs could be, not those floppy one-armed things that most girls gave one another. She set down her drink and sat down with a dramatic sigh. A few actual breast-feeders looked our way, irritated.

"So?" I asked. "How was Thanksgiving? How's your family?"

"Awful," she said. "My parents have been fighting the whole time. They're going to get divorced now that I'm in school. They don't need to hold it together anymore."

"Wow, that's terrible. How are you dealing with it?"

She shrugged. "It's no surprise. They've been like this for a while. I'm just taking it as it comes, you know? I can't predict what's going to happen. Maybe they'll actually just stay together and fight for the rest of their lives."

"That'd be lots of fun," I said.

"You know it. So what is going on with you?"

"What's going on with *you*?" I asked, not-so-subtly dodging her question. "What are you taking? What's your roommate like? How's your dorm? How's the West Coast? All roller skates and avocado?"

"I'm taking taxidermy, fly-fishing, and home ec," she said. "My roommate is a little gnome from Belgravia, and my dorm is actually a cardboard box. We have an earthquake every day."

"Much more interesting than I would have expected."

"Actually, I'm pre-med," she said. "It sucks."

"Since when were you going to be pre-med?" Of all the classes we'd ditch in high school, Kate enjoyed blowing off science the most.

She shrugged. "It was some weird whim. But I'm enjoying it. There's this one class next year, organic chemistry, that makes everyone cry. Everyone. People are lucky to pass with a D in it. I can't wait."

"Well, good luck with that. You're not operating on me."

"I'm afraid you're inoperable anyway." She started rummaging around in her purse, which had begun buzzing, a big cable-knit thing that looked like a sweater with a zipper on it. She pulled out her cell phone, which was actually more like a mini computer. I recognized it from TV commercials.

"Hold on one second," she instructed me and put the device to her ear. "Hey, rock star. What's up? What happened with—are you serious? No way. Well, fuck him, then. Yeah. Listen, can I call you back? I'm out right now. Okay. Bye!" I looked around the coffeehouse while she talked. I didn't know if it was rude for me to stare at her while she had her other conversation or whatever.

"Sorry about that," she said, shoving her device back in her bag. "That was my roommate, Liz. Guy stuff."

"Oh yeah? What's your roommate like?'

"She's great."

"Good!" I hoped I sounded sincere. I would have rather heard stories about a horrible roommate, one who made her own granola and washed her underwear in the sink and hung it to dry all over the room. Or, better yet, a cheerleader. I felt bad wishing that I could hear a few complaining stories from Kate, but it would have made me feel better to offer her some comfort too than to just sit there and listen to how awesome everything was.

"I didn't think I'd like her when we first met. She's from

New York, and at first she seemed, I dunno, Miss Popularity. She already knew, like, twenty people on our floor, and she brought a case of beer with her. I was, like, the two of us have nothing in common. But we got to know each other a little bit more and now she's awesome. Really fun, really smart. We have a good time. I might go with her to her house in the Hamptons this summer."

"Good!" I said again, and suddenly felt a little self-conscious about how greasy my dirty hair felt and the ink stain on my jeans. I crossed one leg under the other. I wished I had something to say that was better than "Well, my roommate has a car and cooks dinner every night" (but Kate already knew that about my dad).

I ended up telling the truth instead of trying to be upbeat and act like things were great. "I don't know what I'm doing, Kate. I don't know what happened. I have no plan. This was not very well thought out. I'm sure that twenty years from now, I'll wish I had learned to play the harmonium or written a book or gone backpacking, but I don't have any desire to do anything. That's what worries me." While I was talking, she pulled a small white patent leather cosmetics case out of her bag and, from that, a white plastic box, which she opened up. She pushed a tiny blue pill through a foil blister pack. She and Germaine looked like they were on the same brand of pill.

"Seeing anyone special?" I asked.

"Sorry," she said. "I have to take these the same time every day and I'm never up early enough to take them in the morning."

"Gotcha," I said.

"And no, not any one particular person," she said.

"Cool," I said. I really didn't feel like talking about boys.

"So anyway, you're too cool for school," she said. "Literally. That's what I think."

"I don't think I'm too anything for school," I said.

"Don't overthink it," she said, looking me in the eye. "I think you'll be fine."

"Oh yeah?" I asked. "How do you know?"

"I don't know," she said. "You should come visit me."

"I should." That would be fun, although I got the impression she didn't totally mean it. Usually when we made plans, it was "Let's go to the House on the Rock *next week*, let's meet at the coffeehouse *tomorrow*, let's hang out *in an hour*."

"You'll be fine," she said again. "You seem fine to me."

"Thanks," I said. "I miss you."

"Hey, remember that time we poured glitter on Hank Thedford's car after he pushed me in the pool senior year?" she asked.

"He was so pissed."

"And his friends called it the FairyMobile." We laughed, but something about this sudden reminiscing felt strange. That had only happened a year ago.

"Hey, that's crazy about Mike, don't you think?" she asked, after a second.

"What are you talking about?" I asked.

"I saw him a few nights ago."

"Where?"

"At the Cellar."

"Oh yeah?"

"Everyone from high school was there the night before Thanksgiving," she said. I looked hard at her.

"Everyone?" *Everyone* used to describe a group of people was one of my pet peeves. Whenever anybody said *Everyone* is going or *Everyone* was there, I was not a part of that *Everyone*.

"Everyone with a fake I.D.," she said, taking a sip from her drink so she didn't have to look at me. My face grew hot, but I guess I couldn't really feel that left out. I wouldn't have been able to get in the stupid bar even if I had wanted to. And I hadn't. But why did Kate even want to go, let alone have an I.D.?

"You have one now?" I asked.

"It's the worst ever. I think that the guys at the bar just let me in because they'd never seen me before."

"Let me see it."

"I lent it to Meg for the rest of the weekend," she said. "Sorry."

One of the reasons I hadn't talked to Meg since junior year was that she accused me of pathetically following Mike around like a puppy. I said, "At least I'm a puppy, not a cow," and we never spoke again. Kate had thought it was pretty funny at the time, especially since she was the one who originally said that Meg seemed sort of cowlike as she moved slowly through the halls at school, making sure everyone got a good look at her huge, braless boobs. I guessed they were friends now.

"Sounds fun," I said, taking a sip of my frothy maple coffee concoction. It was cold by then.

"Anyway, Mike's transferring schools," she said. "The University of Kansas."

"What? Why?"

"To be with Wendy. She goes there."

"He's still with Wendy Maloney?"

"Yeah."

"Wow," I said. "He's transferring from Harvard to . . ."

"Yeah."

"For a girl. From our high school." I could see doing something like that for a really special girl, like maybe a princess, or Oprah, but not old Wendy Maloney. I didn't actually know anything that was technically wrong with Wendy, but I wouldn't leave Harvard to move to Kansas for her.

"Yeah," she said, taking another sip of her drink. "It's sort of romantic."

"Get the fuck out of here! That's not romantic at all! It's stupid," was what I wanted to say. But I didn't. I just took another sip of my cold drink and wondered that maybe since he was also doing something colossally dumb, it wouldn't be that strange talking to Mike after all. It couldn't have felt any odder than talking to Kate, who seemed to have suddenly become possessed. Bits of the old Kate still poked through, but there was something else in there as well.

When we left, she gave me the one-armed hug but also knocked over some kid's Jenga tower, pretending it was an accident. Usually after I hung out with Kate, I felt refreshed, renewed, even inspired to go *do* something. I felt half empty this time, though.

# december

**I had to admit,** the news about Mike intrigued me. Declining to go to college for no good reason seemed like a dumb idea, but transferring from Harvard to the University of Kansas—for a girl—seemed pretty dumb as well. I wondered what was going through Mike's mind. Maybe he needed me as a friend. Maybe I also just needed to talk to him, because I was bored, because I was lonely, because Jane had told me to, because some part of me had to see if what was happening to Kate was also happening to Mike. Each time we'd talked since Thanksgiving, she mentioned some new guy that she had a crush on or was hooking up with (and I learned that "hooking up" in college means "having sex" and not "kissing or anything else" the way it did in high school). It seemed to be a different guy each week. I was having a hard time telling the difference between these guys—or caring. If Mike was also turning into a college clone, then I wouldn't have to think about him anymore.

One day, when both Dad and Germaine were out of the house, I sat down at the desk that was in the dark corner of our kitchen. I needed the quiet to think. I stared at the computer screen hard until I got mad at it for not giving me a sign one way or another what I should do. Then I let my eyes go out of focus as I debated. My brain hurt. It felt like I hadn't really had to think that hard about anything for a while.

Finally, I opened up a new e-mail. *Hey,* I typed. *What's up?*

I hit send before I had time to rethink it. So I wasn't exactly spilling my guts out. But I had finally e-mailed Mike. Now I could quit worrying about whether to e-mail him and start worrying about whether he would write me back, whether he would get the e-mail, or whether he would ignore the e-mail.

Other than the painful-yet-admittedly-kind-of-fun anticipation of waiting to see if Mike would write me back, Christmas was crappy. I honestly don't know why I would have expected it to be otherwise; it wasn't like I had done anything to deserve much more than a lump of coal in my stocking. The year before, I had received lots of stuff to take to college: a new laptop (which Josh ended up appropriating), some reference books that I'd probably never use, little knickknacks for my dorm room. This year, Dad got me a college guide.

"Are you serious?" I asked after I opened the present. We'd had our usual Christmas dinner of Popeye's fried chicken around the dining table and now we were upstairs in the family room, sitting on the couches by the tree (which I had decorated this year in shades of purple and gold) and listening to the cheesy Christmas carols radio station while Superhero went nuts with a pig-ear chew toy. I'd gotten the same book junior year. Only now I had a more up-to-date version. I was rarely that rude, but I couldn't help myself.

"We stop getting more than one present each from Dad after we graduate from high school, remember?" said Josh. "Family policy."

"Oh, was that why you didn't want to go to college?" added Germaine. "Because you didn't want to stop getting presents?"

"Yeah, something like that," I said, staring at Dad, who was watching the floor, swirling around the one glass of expensive Scotch he let himself have per year. I was pissed. I was annoyed at myself for being pissed, because I felt like I was too old to be mad about what I got or didn't get for Christmas. But it wasn't really that. I didn't like passive-aggressive hints. He had been doing things lately like leaving me clippings from newspapers about picking the right college, or how many great amenities freshmen were getting lately. I'd rather he pound a huge drum and stomp around the house chanting "Back to school, back to school" than this.

"Well, thanks," I said, putting it aside.

"Your mom sent over some stuff," said Dad, pointing to a big black shiny shopping bag next to the tree. This had better be a redeeming present or else I was giving up Christmas forever. Inside the bag was a black leather jacket from Italy. Admittedly, it was pretty cool, but it certainly wouldn't be warm enough in Chicago to wear anytime soon. Also included was a cardboard tube. I could tell that the jacket was going to be clothing when I saw the box, but this was a surprise.

"What is it?" I asked.

"I don't know!" said Dad, while Josh and Germaine tried on their jackets. We didn't mind if we all got the same present from her, because if it was good, we all got something good, and if it was bad, we could all complain together.

I pulled the metal cap out of one side of the tube and extracted a big poster. It was so huge that when I spread my arms to see it, it still didn't open up all the way. We had to put two mugs from our hot chocolate down on the ends to see what it was.

"Sexy," said Josh. It was a black-and-white photo of a couple kissing in some café. I think it was French. The café, not the kissing.

"What is this?"

"There's a card," Dad said, handing me a business card with some scrawling on the back.

*For your dorm!!!! Xoxox,* Mom had written on it.

"That's great," I said. "She doesn't remember that I'm not in college."

"Maybe it's for when you go back," said Josh.

"If you go back," said Germaine.

I stood up. "Where do we keep the wine?" I asked, picking up one of the mugs and letting the poster roll back up with a snap. "I need a drink."

"Shut up," said Dad.

● ● ●

I left the college book in the family room for a few days, hoping that maybe somebody would make it disappear. I would rather get a booster shot and my teeth cleaned simultaneously than have to look at, and apply to, colleges again.

A few days after Christmas, I woke to the smell of waffles cooking: Dad sometimes made special breakfasts for us while we were all on break. Of course I wasn't really on Christmas break, but I was happy to enjoy the benefits of Dad's and Josh's. I wandered downstairs in my sweatpants and T-shirt and found the table set, with the dreaded college guide on my plate. Cute.

"What is this?" I asked. "Where are my waffles?"

"This is a trap," Dad said, talking above the radio set to NPR, which he always listened to too loudly. "To get you to look at schools again. You need to at least start thinking about what's going to happen this summer."

"This summer," I said, "it's going to be hot. Perhaps a thunderstorm or two."

"You're going back to school," he said, pointing his spatula at me. "We just have to face facts and get to it, unless you want to have a big fight over it."

"Don't point that thing at me," I said. He poked me with it instead and put down a plate of waffles with whipped cream and strawberries.

"Enjoy!"

I sat down and flipped through the book while I ate my fancy waffles. The kitchen had seemed so bright and clean and happy and welcoming, especially the sunshine bouncing off the fresh snow in the yard, but it was all a horrible mirage.

**december**

These college guides are supposed to help you make an educated decision about what schools you are interested in based on several factors, such as size, location, and academic strengths and weaknesses. But in reality everybody just reads them to find out how the food is or what the party scene is like. I read a description of one school that called the town it was located in "One of the Seven Gates of Hell." If that's not intriguing, I don't know what is.

My vision began to blur as I stared at the book. It described colleges in the most boring way possible:

> The "Christian Path" is considered an essential component of the university's curriculum. . . .

Too religious. I hadn't been in a church since the last time my mom pulled me into one in Europe to look at the frescoes.

> Inherently, the student body is issue-oriented. Students spend a good deal of time in the library. It's also joked that each professor believes that you're majoring in his or her subject. Approximately 70 percent of each graduating class moves into the job market after matriculation. . . .

Too boring. And with lame jokes.

> There are no core requirements: students are encouraged to create their own majors, with mandatory enrollment in at least four areas of study at all times. All students must take classes in the fine arts, social sciences, natural sciences, and humanities.

Too intimidatingly brainy.

*The student body eagerly looks forward to key social events each year that attract swarms of men.*
Too many women.

*Dedicated environmentalists abound. . . .*
Too good. Too many hippies.

*Approximately 75 percent of the student body go Greek, and those who avoid the Greek system tend to feel excluded from the social scene.*
Too horrible to even consider.

After about fifteen minutes, I put my head on the kitchen table, wondering how bad Dad would feel if I were found dead like that. The book was giving me a headache. I groaned.

"Nice try," Dad said, taking my plate from me. "But you're not going to get off the hook anymore. I want you to think about this, Cecily. Fun time is over."

"When was fun time?" I asked. "I must have missed that." I started heading up the stairs.

"I'm serious," he said. "Come here." And I walked halfway back down the stairs.

"What?" I said snottily. "I have to go upstairs and research schools."

"Come *here*," he repeated, pointing to the floor. I rolled my eyes. I hated feeling like this, like I was ten.

"You're going back to school. If it's not going to be Kenyon, you'd better figure out which school it is going to be. We're going to have to fill out applications, go to interviews, the whole shebang—all over again. And by 'we,' I mean you, because I don't have time to go over it all again, but I do have time to make you do it yourself."

I rolled my eyes again.

"Also, I called Kenyon and talked to the admissions office after we came back last fall. They said it's okay if you want to come back, because I originally told them that you were just deferring enrollment."

"Oh," I said. "Thanks." I somehow felt betrayed. I was so used to not doing anything with this year that it felt like an invasion that he had done anything productive without me knowing it.

"But if you decide that you don't want to go to Kenyon, that's fine. You just have to figure it out now so I can let them know you're not going there. That's why I got you the book."

I moaned. The last thing I wanted was choices. "All right, Dad," I said. "I'll let you know in a few weeks."

"Days."

"Fine," I said. "Sounds good. See you later."

I started back up the stairs, and, for some reason, seeing Germaine's closed door made me stop. I went back halfway down the stairs.

"Dad?"

"Yes, baby?"

"How come you let me stay here? This year?"

"I thought you wanted to stay here."

"Yeah. But . . . how come you didn't *make* me go?"

"I don't make monkeys," he said, and made a face.

"Funny."

• • •

Conrad and Germaine were watching a movie in the living room. I was sure that they wouldn't mind if I joined them as I looked through the college guide book more. Germaine rolled her eyes several times and mouthed a few variations of "Get out," but I pretended not to see.

"What are some things that I want in a college?" I wondered aloud.

Conrad perked up. "Do you want activism? Do you want to do community service? Do you want to study abroad? Do you want a campus friendly to the gay/lesbian/bisexual/transgendered community? A medieval society?"

I stared at him. I'd never heard him speak so much in his life. And he wasn't making any sense.

"Huh?"

"Choosing a college is one of the most important steps you'll ever take in your life. It will affect who your friends are, what your interests are, where you find a job, who your lovers are. What sort of organizations you might be interested in, what activities, study options. It can really help define who you will be. I can help you if you want."

Define who I would be? I now wanted to not be here, not having this conversation. Germaine stared at me so hard, I got a little scared.

"Where did you originally go?" he asked.

"She went to Kenyon," Germaine said.

"Oh, you went to Kenyon?" he repeated.

"For about five minutes," I said. "Actually, maybe more like two hours."

"That's a good school," Conrad said. "I had some friends there. Did you know Todd Turkowitz?"

"Did I!" I exclaimed. "He was like my best friend there! We'd have ever so much fun. We would laugh and laugh."

"Don't listen to her," said Germaine.

"Thank you so much, Conrad. This has been most helpful. I will be sure to come to you if I have any further questions. Good day." I tipped an imaginary cap and walked out of the room.


Germaine and I were still annoying the shit out of each other, so it was nice having Josh back for Christmas, just because he seemed glad to be home, which made the house feel a little happier in general. I was not terribly happy, though, when we heard that his girlfriend was coming to visit. I was pretty sure her name was Angie, but I couldn't be positive. (Actually, I knew it was Angie, but I kept pretending that I forgot it whenever I talked about her to Dad or Germaine. Neither of them found this amusing.)

Josh and I had never really hung out, just the two of us, outside the house. In fact, he'd sort of ignored me at the beginning of high school, which was devastating at the time. He apologized later, saying that he was just trying to fit in with his friends, but it took me a while to get over the first few days of school, yelling "Hey, J-baby!" (Mom's nickname for him) in the hall only to have him walk by and not even look at me.

But we have gotten along fine ever since. I wasn't sure how Josh ended up seeming so much more easygoing than Germaine and me. Who knows, maybe he was full of secret turmoil and he just managed to act like nothing bothered him too much. But he didn't seem to get irritated by Dad the way Germaine always did, and when I heard him on the phone with Mom, he didn't seem to hate talking to her the way I did.

So I wasn't sure what it was that I distrusted so much about this girlfriend, but I knew that Josh had been a little annoying since he'd gotten home for break, squirreling away in his room and talking on the phone and making stupid giggly noises, so I had to assume she was the cause of it all. Plus, Yolanda had to come an extra day during the week to clean for the houseguest, which put me in a bad mood because whenever Yolanda cleaned, she moved my stuff from where my stuff needed to be. I had very specific piles around my room that meant certain things. These I would file at a later time. These would get thrown away on Tuesday. This one would just stay around for a while. She consolidated them all, and it drove me wild.

I knew that Angie was coming the day before New Year's Eve, so to avoid the grand entrance, I hid in our local Barnes & Noble, which was a bad plan since the store was full of kids off from school and people returning gifts. I bought a celebrity trash magazine and sat in the corner of the café with my back to the room, so if anybody from my school came in, they wouldn't see me. Eventually I finished the magazine, and I felt that if I ordered another hot chocolate, my teeth would fall out of my head, so I headed home.

I just had to stay out of the common areas of the house where Josh and Angie might be hanging out. I didn't want to know what they were doing, but I imagined they were staring at each other and sighing in adoration.

When I came home, Dad was in the kitchen, paying some bills.

"Angie's here," he said, smiling.

"Oh yeah? What's she like?"

"She seems really cool."

*"Cool?"*

"She definitely doesn't seem like she's in a bad mood, unlike you. I might trade her for you."

"Look, I can't promise I'll be in a good mood, but what if I just keep my bad mood away from them?"

"That's fine," he said. "Just be polite. Are you jealous or something?"

"No," I said. "I just don't like people in my personal space."

"I guess it's a bad idea that I told her she could sleep in your bed," he said.

"Ha-ha." I went upstairs to brush the chocolate taste out of my mouth. When I stepped out of the bathroom I saw my brother smooching somebody blond and petite in the hallway. I figured that people who make out prefer to do it on couches or beds or in bars, but anywhere seemed to do in the case of these two perverts.

"Hi." I tried to sound like this was all perfectly normal, that I was cool with running into weird makeout sessions. Even Germaine had the decency to close the door when she and Conrad did the disgusting things they did. My brother blushed, but the blond person looked up and smiled.

"Cecily, right? I'm Angie! It's so nice to meet you." She marched toward me with her hand held out. She gripped mine, perfectly firm. If I were giving her a job interview, I would have hired her on the spot, based on the handshake. She wore a red sweater that somehow showed off her small waist and looked comfy and warm, too. I never knew where girls found such sweaters.

I glanced at Josh, but he was busy staring at Angie with big, wet, shiny, adoring cow eyes. I wanted to puke.

"Nice to meet you, too," I said. I think that's what you said in situations like this. You lied.

"Were you out returning Christmas presents?" she asked.

"I wish," I said. "I wish I had presents I could return." She laughed loud.

"This is Angie's first time to Chicago," said Josh.

"Oh," I said. "Well, I hope you like it."

"I do," she said. "Josh and I are going to go to the Art Institute in a little bit."

"Oh really?" I turned to Josh.

"Why 'oh really'?" Angie asked, as Josh looked at the ground.

"This one time Dad tried to take all three of us to the Art Institute, Josh was so determined not to see any art that he sat in the car the entire time we were there. Even though Dad promised he'd get us all something from the gift shop. And even though we parked in an underground garage."

"So you didn't have a book or anything?" asked Angie.

"No," said Josh.

"You were that determined not to see art?"

He shrugged. "What can I say? I thought it was lame."

"How long ago was this?" Angie asked.

"It was last week," I said. She laughed again. After they left, I had the sinking feeling that it was going to be really hard to hate Angie, so I went and bugged Germaine to get off the computer and let me check my e-mail, even though I knew I didn't have any.

"I'm using it," she said.

"Dad, Germaine won't let me use the computer," I called to his office, in a voice I had perfectly pitched so that I knew he couldn't hear it but she'd think he could.

"Jesus Christ," she said. "Have it. God."

That felt much more natural.


Angie ate dinner with us, although Germaine had escaped by going to Conrad's place. He shared a dumpy apartment in the city with five other guys, and Germaine only went there in the direst of circumstances, like when she had to be pleasant to houseguests. Dad was fascinated by Angie and wanted to know what she thought about the Art Institute, since she had just finished an art history class at school and he'd minored in that when he was in college.

Angie seemed all right. But something about the way she was so friendly yet polite was almost *professional*. Or too adult. Or too happy. I felt like she was an actor pretending to be somebody who was twenty instead of an actual twenty-year-old. She just seemed so damned nice and polite, and I kept waiting for her to turn into Germaine, or Kate, or any of the other girls I knew who had gone to college. Secretly she had to be fake, or boring, or a bitch. Even though it wasn't fair of me to assume this, I kept expecting the transformation to happen. I was just nervous being around someone, too, whom I had to behave around.

"We rented some movies tonight if you want to watch them with us," said Josh. "*Ghostbusters* and *What About Bob?*. Some Bill Murray stuff in honor of Angie's first time in Chicago."

"Sounds like fun," I said. Sitting around watching movies with them sounded awkward.

"I'm going to hang out and watch them, too, Cecily," said Dad. "You should join us." I tried to think of any reason I could not watch the movies with them that didn't involve me sitting awkwardly and quietly in my room, not doing anything. But I had no plans, nobody to call.

"I got some ice cream," added Dad.

"Okay," I finally consented. What can I say, I like ice cream. Who doesn't?

Upstairs with our ice cream, as *What About Bob?* began, I kept sneaking glances at Angie. It was weird being in close proximity to another girl, one who wasn't my sister, our cleaning lady, or my mother. She ate her ice cream without looking at it, just sticking her spoon into the blue ceramic bowl and lifting it to her mouth. She wasn't messy or anything, but she didn't take care to parcel out tiny portions of ice cream into her spoon the way Germaine did, didn't wipe her mouth constantly the way Mom did. Her hair was really blond, unlike Germaine's, which was sort of dirty blond. It was pulled back in a ponytail with little pieces falling perfectly around her face. She had a little turned-up nose and big brown eyes. In order to have an excuse to stare at her, I started talking.

"So how did you and Josh meet?"

"He stalked me," she said. "For a year."

"I had a Dante class with her that I couldn't stand, but she told me she was signing up for a Chaucer class, and I did it, just so I could hang out with her," Josh said.

"Finally, at the end of the term, he told me that he was only doing it so he could study with me. So I told him to go screw himself."

"And she kicked me in the groin!"

"Wow," I said. "That's cute."

I shut up, and we went back to the movie. I liked that Angie laughed at the movie, loudly and without waiting to see if we were laughing, too. I had always thought the movie was okay, but I never enjoyed it as much as I did watching it with Angie.

I had another appointment with Jane coming up, so I decided to go the extra mile and try calling Kate again. We had been speaking less and less often, or actually, she was. I had been leaving voice mails and e-mails—not any more than I usually would have, but I felt like a pathetic stalker. Without her, I'd have no friends to talk to and I knew that wouldn't be good. We had meant to get together while she was home for Christmas, but the one time that we made an actual plan, she had canceled, citing "family plans," which I thought was total bullshit. I had never heard of her canceling fun to do something with her family, especially if her parents were on the verge of killing each other. My hands shook when I dialed. Stupid Kate.

"What's up?" she asked when she picked up the phone. They had caller I.D. in her room, which had been making me paranoid.

"How's school?" I came up with lamely, after running out of preliminary conversation.

"School is cool," she said. "It's cool to be in school. And follow the rules. And drool. While wearing mules."

"Shut up." I didn't even have a clever comeback.

"Seriously, things are going good." She started telling me about some guy named Greg that she had been e-mailing me about. He was really cute. He was in her Spanish class.

"So, we kind of hooked up on Thursday night at happy hour."

"Now, is he the one who lives on your floor? The football guy?"

"No, the football guy and I were just friends. That's Quinn. The other guy on my floor is Randy, and we don't speak anymore. That was just a one-time thing. He has a girlfriend anyway."

"Ah, I see."

"Actually, they're having some kind of Round-the-World party thing outside in my hall right now, so I have to go. See you!"

"What's a Round-the-World party?" I asked, but Kate had already hung up. A Round-the-World party, as I later found out, is an excuse to get drunk. Everything in college that is not class is an excuse to get drunk, it seems. St. Patrick's Day is an excuse to get drunk. The fifth of May is an excuse to get drunk. A warm day is an excuse to get drunk. A Round-the-World party is just another one, only in this case people wear togas and yarmulkes and sombreros.

Kate and I tried to get drunk once or twice in high school, not because we were going anywhere special, but almost as an experiment. We wanted to see what it was like, if it was really that great. One time, she slept over at my house, and we took a bottle of kiwi-strawberry Snapple, crept downstairs to Dad's sparse liquor shelf in the kitchen, and put about a drop of vodka in the bottle. We shared sips, watching *Saturday Night Live* and giggling together about what we'd act like once we got drunk (start beating each other up? cry and call ex-lovers?), but not surprisingly, we didn't get drunk. We tried it again another night at her house, with the same flavor of Snapple, only we added her mother's rum. A lot of it. Probably too much, because after a few sips we agreed it tasted bad and poured it down the toilet.

I really never got drinking. I guess my parents had unwittingly sabotaged that whole thing, since I had been around alcohol my whole life. Not that either one of them was a big boozer, but they just didn't treat it like it was anything too special. Dad would have a drink of wine every now and then and Mom, when she lived with us, liked her Manhattans, and I thought both tasted like crap. I much preferred to sneak sips from Dad's creamy, sugary coffee.

I tried to get drunk; I just never got there. I'd get tired before I got to the giggly, laughing point that my friends did. I remember one particular Christmas dance. Meg had smuggled a bottle of white wine from her parents' house over to Kate's, and Meg swigged from it as we got ready for the night. I remember that it was the sophomore-year dance, because I let Kate do my makeup and was surprised that she actually did a good job—she did something with some eyeliner that made my eyes look fascinatingly gray and not that drab-gray that was too indecisive to be blue or green.

I also let her do my hair, some twisty thing she had accomplished so that I had little tendrils along the sides. Who knew that Kate had such skills? I had expected her to make me look like a cartoon character. I guess we got too into it because Meg sat on the toilet (seat down) the whole time and drank from her bottle, and by the time we left she had drunk almost the whole thing, which we didn't realize until we got back.

At the dance, we acted stupid as usual, shaking our butts on the dance floor in inexpensive formal wear, and Meg began throwing herself around harder and harder.

"Do you think Jaash likes me?" she yelled in my ear. My brother had graduated from our high school the year before.

"No," I said. I was positive that Josh didn't even know who she was.

"Shut up!" she squealed, and slapped me across the arm, hard. "I think he's sooooo haaht," she said, and this time I could smell her hot breath, and it smelled like ass.

"Hey, is she okay?" yelled Kate.

Meg rested her hand heavily on my shoulder to tell me something else that I'm sure was very important, but she fell down, bringing me to the floor with her. She screamed with laughter, and I tried to pretend to laugh along with her, but soon she dissolved into tears.

"What is wrong with you?" I asked, even though I knew what was wrong with her.

"Nobody luh-huh-hoves me," she blubbered. Kate and some of our other friends came over and were trying to pick her up, but Meg was playing the wet noodle game with her bones and felt like she weighed three hundred pounds.

"We gotta get her out of here before she barfs all over the place," Kate said. "Or before she gets in trouble."

"Or before people start sliding around in her barf," I said. We started giggling and then laughing. For some reason, the deejay made the music even louder at that point, so we couldn't hear anything, not our laughing, not Meg's groaning, just Sir Mix-a-Lot's approval of big butts.

We eventually hustled Meg to the gym exit and found a cab. Kate and I had to do rock-paper-scissors for who was going to sit with her in the backseat, and I won, for the first time in my entire life (scissors). Kate propped up Meg against the window behind the cabbie so he couldn't see her, sticking her mouth and nose out like a dog so that her little bursts of clear puke would slide down the outside of the window. The driver didn't notice, or at least he pretended not to.

Maybe getting drunk in college was different from getting drunk in high school. Everyone in college seemed to do it, it seemed. Everyone expected that you'd do it, so maybe it was more . . . what? I didn't know. It was more relaxing? You weren't as worried about getting caught? You didn't have to do it in such a hurry? It made you charming and delightful, as opposed to barfy?

After the night of the Round-the-World party, I tried calling Kate a few more times. She was so busy with classes and a fun new boy named Adam that as our talks grew fewer and farther between, it was harder to catch up. Our conversations would have to be an hour long for me to hear everything she was up to. When I called, I usually got either her roommate or their voice mail, which consisted of them singsonging that they weren't home. Even though I didn't know her at all, I grew to hate the roommate, with her loud voice and New York accent that, I'm sorry, sounded fake. Otherwise, Kate was just using that caller I.D. and wasn't picking up because she didn't want to talk to her stupid former friend who was too much of a baby to leave home.

For New Year's, Josh and Angie ended up going down to Navy Pier to watch the fireworks. Germaine was out with Conrad. I realized that this was a good reason for me to be talking to my friends, the way Jane had recommended. I had no plans, and while I didn't mind sitting at home with Dad on any other night, tonight just seemed extra pathetic. I told Dad that Kate and I were going to a party, even though I knew she was going out in the city with some friends from college. He seemed so happy that he offered to give me cab money. I promised him I wouldn't touch any alcohol and borrowed the car. I spent the night slowly driving up and down the lakeshore, through the towns that got richer and smaller the farther north I went. I listened to music and sang to myself and would feel pretty hollow when certain songs would come on, and I felt like if life were a music video, I'd be crying beautifully at that moment, but it wasn't and I didn't, not at all. I brought myself home around one o'clock, when I knew Dad would be asleep already. The next morning, I told him that Kate and I didn't go out; we just stayed in and watched movies. He didn't question me further.

# january

**I was aware** of how pitiful my New Year's Eve was, so I made one resolution for myself: get out of the house more. Surely good things lay for me outside our door! New friends! Inspiration! Perhaps a model scout who would say, "You are clearly too short for this job, but you have a certain I-don't-know-what. Are you in school? No? Good, come with me!"

Yes, getting out would solve everything.

The problem with that was, once I had promised myself to do so, it felt like a huge imposition. Dad had gotten me a membership at the university gym after I complained that the groceries I carried in from the car were too heavy, and for the first few days of the new year, I dutifully put on my workout clothes and then sat around waiting for an excuse not to go out: snow, a really good rerun on TV, the need for a nap. After a few days, Dad pointed out that it was pretty crappy of me not to use the membership that he had paid for, so the first

Friday of the new year, I promised myself I was really, really going to go. As soon as this episode of *What's Happening!!* was over. Then the phone rang.

"Hello?" I answered, expecting that it would be for Dad or Germaine. I had gotten used to being their secretary. I didn't mind it. I liked practicing my handwriting as I took down messages.

"Hey there," said a friendly guy's voice.

"Uh," I said smoothly. Who the hell was this? Then my heart sped up. It was Mike.

"Hi," he said again.

"Um, how are you?"

"Fine," he said. "How are you?"

"Good," I said.

"Good," he said. I still couldn't get my head around the fact that Mike had called. He hadn't e-mailed me back after I had written him. That first week, I checked my e-mail compulsively. The week after that, I felt hideously embarrassed that I had been so foolish as to actually e-mail Mike. The week after that, I told myself to forget it, that I wasn't friends with Mike after all, and that who cared anyway. By last week, I had almost forgotten about the whole thing. Now this.

"I got your e-mail," he said. "But honestly I didn't feel like typing everything down that's new. And I don't know what you know. So I put it off. But I'm home now. I'm going back after break in a few days. So I figured we could just talk."

"Okay," I said.

"You're not a real treat to talk to on the phone, do you know that?"

"I hate the phone," I said. "A phone killed my mother."

"Shut up," he said. "Want to come over tonight?"

"Sure," I said. "I'll call you later after dinner."

"Yeah, you will," he said, and hung up.

I turned off the TV. That thinking feeling again. I used to go over to Mike's house all the time in high school before he started seeing Wendy. It was no big deal. We'd sit in his small bedroom on the blue carpet and look up old music videos online or play records and talk, sometimes just sit there in silence and listen to whatever he put on. The door was always open, and his mom would walk by sometimes, doing laundry, occasionally stopping to chat. It felt good to be around her, too, a short-haired, rather big-butted mom who seemed fine with being a mom, not trying to impress anyone with her fabulousness. Was any of it going to be the same? Why did I feel nervous? I went to the gym and had to quit jogging after just two laps around the track because I felt like I was going to throw up.

"I'm going over to Mike's later," I announced over dinner. Germaine looked up.

"Oh yeah?" said Dad. If I knew him, he was trying not to look surprised or excited or happy as he served himself some salad. "Tell him we miss him."

"I don't miss him," said Germaine.

"Tell him I miss him and Germaine doesn't," said Dad.

"Will do," I said. I kept pushing around the thin piece of breaded veal on my plate, trying to decide if I should change out of my ancient brown thrift-store corduroys or put on some makeup or something before I went over. I didn't do that before. I didn't know why I wanted to now. I decided that I wouldn't change anything.

I drove to Mike's house, an exactly five-minute drive as always, and parked outside. The driveway was empty, so his parents were probably out.

He opened the door before I got to it.

"Dang, you know how much I love ringing doorbells," I said, walking up the cobblestone path, which lay in a swervy line for some reason. "Thus explaining my dream to be a door-to-door doorbell salesman."

"Hello, Cecily," he said, and opened his arms up wide for a hug. I wrapped my arms around his middle. He felt thicker. Not fat, but more solid. Or something? Maybe my arms were hallucinating.

"Want something to drink?" he asked as I closed the door behind me. I took off my peacoat and hung it in the hall closet. It felt like it had been forever since I used to act like his house was my own. He looked pretty damn good. He had cut his hair quite short, and it looked thick and shiny. It had been a few years since he had had short hair, and now it showed off what was almost a pretty-boy face. His dark eyebrows and light green eyes made him look sensitive, almost sad, although that wasn't the case, at least with the old Mike I knew, anyway.

"Do you guys have any hot chocolate?" I asked. "I like the hair, by the way."

"I think so, and thanks," he said as we walked to the kitchen. I sat at the dark gray marble counter in the middle of their snug kitchen as he rummaged through the cabinets.

"So, what have you heard?" he asked, pulling out a tin of Ghirardelli hot chocolate. Score.

"What have I heard about what?" I asked. "I've heard many things, Mike. Children laughing. Birds singing. Cars backfiring."

"I mean how much have you heard from other people about my year thus far?" he said. "I'm sure some people have told other people."

"Kate told me a few things," I said. "Like how you got pregnant and they kicked you out of school. Oh Mike, how could you."

"Ha-ha," he said, filling up the teakettle with water. I actually wanted milk in the hot chocolate. "We're out of milk," he said, as if he read my mind. Creepy.

"Seriously, I heard that you left Harvard to transfer to the University of Kansas to be with a girl," I said. He looked down and smirked at the teakettle. I'd forgotten how he hung his head and smirked, letting his hair shag down around his eyebrows, when he got embarrassed. Now his hair didn't cover his eyes. "I don't know if that's true or not, though. We don't have to talk about it, you know. It's none of my business."

"That's nice of you," he said, and pulled a comically large mug from the cabinet overhead. "Seriously. Most people so far either act like they didn't hear about it when clearly they did, or they just ask, 'How could you do that?' Like I murdered someone."

"Well, I don't know what you heard about me," I said.

"How you took the year off?" he said.

"Good news travels fast," I said.

He sat down on the other side of the bar. I felt like we were in a coffee commercial. "So," he said. "So what. Picking a school and just going to it is lame, right?" The kettle began to shriek.

"Hey, can we hang out in your room?" I said suddenly. "It just feels like it would be more normal."

"I'm not going to have sex with you, Cecily, if that's what you're hoping," he said, lowering his head and staring at me hard. We had never talked about sex before in our lives. We weren't that kind of close. It felt like I was talking to Mike's randier older brother, if he'd had one. At the very least, I wished he would stop calling me by my name.

"Fine," I said. "I'm not having sex with you." Maybe I was remembering it wrong, but when we were closer in high school, it felt like I did most of the joking and teasing while Mike just tolerated it.

"I'm kidding," he said. "Fine, we'll go upstairs." He poured three huge scoops of the cocoa mix into the mug, added some water, stirred it with a spoon, and handed it to me. I thought Mike, after being more of a quiet guy all those years, had suddenly developed a little attitude. Unless I had turned into a social idiot around him all of a sudden. It was possible both things had happened.

"All right," he said, settling down on the floor of his room. "You happy now?"

"Almost," I said, and grabbed our high school yearbook off his shelf. I had to have something in my hands. And the hot chocolate was still too hot. "I'm going to laugh at the things people have signed here."

"Be my guest," said Mike. "Hold on a second." He was the only person I knew on the planet who bought and played LPs. He put on an old Beck album.

"Are you still playing guitar?" I asked.

"Haven't had the time," he said. "Plus, you know, the college guy strumming alone in his dorm room thing. I don't want to be that guy."

"Yeah, that guy would be weird," I said. I didn't know of said guy, but I could sort of imagine it.

"It's just not my thing anymore, you know?" he said. I admired that he could say that he had a "thing" and then he didn't. I didn't even know if I had a thing to begin with, let alone not. Maybe not going to school was my thing?

"So what have you been doing so far?" Mike asked, taking a seat on the carpet. He leaned against the bed. I leaned against the opposite wall. We could have had a pretty good kicking match if we wanted to. The music was just the right mix of melodic and weird, stuff I'd never listen to on my own but was perfect for hanging out.

*To Miguel—It was fun sitting next to you in Spanish. Sí. That's all I can remember, can you believe that? —Erin*

I sighed. "Like, nothing. I haven't even been doing any thinking."

"I doubt that."

"Well, I feel like I have to justify this year somehow and I haven't. So I've mostly been sitting around getting pissed at everyone."

"Better than having everyone be pissed at you."

"Who says they aren't?"

*Mike—You're amazing. I know you'll go far. Don't be a stranger! XOXOXOX Tracy*

"Maybe we should have a fight over whose parent is more pissed at them right now—your dad or my parents," Mike said.

"I think you'd win," I said. "My dad is mad—well, I don't know if he's mad. I don't know what he is."

"I still can't get over how angry my mom and dad were," he said, rubbing his eyebrow with his ring finger. "Things are just starting to get a little more normal since we've been spending some more time around one another."

"That bad, huh?"

"Here's what happened. In October, I told them I couldn't take being without Wendy anymore and was transferring to UK. I had already taken care of the paperwork and everything. They didn't speak to me until they were on campus three days later. They got me in their hotel room at nine A.M. and wouldn't quit yelling at me literally until nine P.M. We actually ordered room service so they wouldn't have to yell at me in public."

"That's incredible."

*You have an odd aroma. I will not hold it against you. —Kate*

"And then Wendy and I broke up."

"Oh really?"

"All my mom could do was laugh when I told her Wendy and I were breaking up. Not in a mean way. I mean, I had to laugh, too. It was almost like a joke when I called her. 'Hey, Ma, you're never going to believe this.'"

"Why did you guys break up?" I realized that I knew nothing about Wendy. I had had a few classes with her in high school. She seemed all right. Bland. She had played soccer, so she hung with the sporty-girl crowd that I didn't know very well.

*Mike—Well, you know . . . —Meg*

This was written in huge slanty letters in bright red ink, taking up a big corner of the inside cover.

"This is going to make me sound like an asshole," he said. "But right when I got there, I realized that it wasn't going to work out. Once I arrived, it was only about an hour before I said, 'I transferred from *Harvard* to be here with you!' I didn't want to be a jerk, but I did feel mad, disappointed. I thought I was being a great guy and this would really change the trajectory of my life. I was excited all the way, and then that first night on campus that we spent together, I was just like, 'Oh great.'" Mike sighed and laughed, sat forward, and then let himself fall back against the side of the bed. "It was dumb," he continued, after we had listened to a few seconds of music. "Really dumb. I don't know. But it's kind of funny to me, too. I don't know, what can I do, you know?" he said, looking at me and then looking back straight ahead. "I won't lie: I'm still freaked out. I'm in *Kansas*, for God's sake. But," he said, and leaned back up, looking me in the eye again, "I'd probably do it again."

A chill went through me. Looking at him, for a second, he seemed like a totally different person. He looked older than me; he looked like, well, a man—a young man—and not my guy friend from high school. I could imagine walking past him on the street, thinking he was older than me, not considering him my age but someone off doing more important things. It freaked me out, seeing him like that. But it was kind of thrilling, too.

"You'd really do it again? I mean, if you meet another girl at Kansas and *she* wants to transfer to the University of Hawaii, you'll go there? When will it end, Mike? Oh when will it ever, ever end?"

"Shut the eff up," he said, kicking me. "I just mean, if I had that same chance again, I probably would have done the same thing."

*Mike—This feels weird, writing in here. Everything feels like it's too obvious to write down. So can I just say, "Have a great summer"? I love you. —Wendy*

"So you seem okay with it," I said. "Good for you."

"I wouldn't say *good for me*," he said. "It wasn't a bright move. I'm not, like, happy I did it. But I just don't want to freak out about it anymore. I'm still really bummed about Wendy."

"Huh, yeah," I said, not wanting to talk about Wendy.

"Besides," he said, "maybe this is just the way that things

were supposed to go anyway. Maybe I would be a total nothing at Harvard, but in the end I'll be a superstar at Kansas."

"I guess it just depends on whether a superstar at Kansas is still better than a nothing at Harvard," I said, and then regretted it. To create a distraction, I took out my elastic and redid my ponytail.

"Your hair's gotten long," Mike said. Distraction accomplished.

"Has it?" I actually hadn't noticed it, but I guess it had been a long time since I'd gotten it cut, probably right before that drive to Kenyon. It was usually about shoulder length when I had it down, which was not often, because it was curly and I didn't feel like bothering to make it look not freakishly frizzy. I pulled it down and could see that it was hanging below my shoulders. I wondered how long my nails would have grown if I'd stopped cutting them as well. I'd look like a crazy mountain hermit man.

"I wonder if I can make a beard out of this," I said, pulling the ends up under my nose.

"You look like Chewbacca," Mike said.

"I bet you wouldn't have conversations like this at Harvard. Deep serious ones."

*To Mike—Have a nice summer. You seem nice. Cecily.*
*P.S. If you can't remember in 20 years that this is a joke entry, then I never knew you.*

"You're right," Mike said. "I made the right choice." I felt bad for him, for putting himself on the line like that and maybe not making the right choice. But at least he had a plan, a reason for doing what he did. And I could tell he would be a superstar no matter where he ended up. Jesus Christ, I can't believe I hung out with him so much and never realized how amazing he is. Maybe things would go well for me, too, I thought. I put the yearbook back on the shelf and, without thinking, ran my hand across all the spines so they lined up. I glanced at him to see if he noticed—he was watching me but didn't say anything, didn't raise an eyebrow or smirk.

"So did you have a hard time?" I asked. "I mean, meeting friends and stuff? During the transfer?"

"Not really," he said. "I think it's almost harder *not* to make friends in college. It's programmed that way, practically. You really have to go out of your way to avoid meeting new people."

"Meeting new people isn't the same as having friends," I pointed out.

"Are you scared of not having any friends?" he said. "Don't worry about it. You'll be fine. You have friends now, right?'

"Barely," I said. "I mean—"

"Get over it," he said. "I'm your friend, right?"

"Maybe I can walk around with a button that says 'Has at least one friend!' on it."

"There you go. But why wouldn't you make friends with people? You're funny. You're fun. You're creative."

"I think I just hung out with funny, fun, creative people. Because I'm not feeling very funny, fun, or creative right now."

"You just need to find people like that, then, and get associated with them."

"Easy!" I said. "Thanks, Mike!"

"So do you think you'll go back?" he asked.

"I don't know," I said. "Maybe. Probably. I still don't have any idea why I'm suddenly so defective."

He shrugged. "You can cultivate an aura of mystery about you. You're inexplicable and you can't be pigeonholed and no institution can tie you down!"

"I don't think that's true."

"Nobody knows that, though. When I got to UK, people had already heard about me. I felt like explaining to them, 'Actually, I'm more than just the guy who transferred here from Harvard to be with a girl,' but in the meantime, hey, at least they thought something about me. And it's a good story to tell at a party."

"So I just need to get invited to some parties," I said.

"Good luck with that."

My hot chocolate had finally cooled off enough to drink, and I decided to go home soon. I was worried about staying up too late, getting too chatty, trying to share too much, and looking foolish. Even though Mike and I had been left alone in his house or my house together several times, I was aware for the first time that I was alone with a guy in a while. I was afraid of staring at his face too much. I was afraid of acting strangely and getting called out on it. But I was glad that I saw him. He was still my friend. I couldn't fuck that up.

"I don't want to put pressure on you," I said when we were at the front door. "But you have to keep in touch. Not all the time. Not even that frequently. But just . . . sometimes. Because if I don't talk to you, I'm not talking to anyone."

"What about Kate?"

"Kate's changed."

"She seems like she's coming out of her shell to me," said Mike.

"I didn't even think that she had a shell," I said. "But seriously. Only friend. Obligation."

"I have to tell you, it takes a lot of balls to be that pitiful," said Mike. Mean but true.

"Just send me the occasional e-mail or call me, will you?" I said. "I'll try calling Kate, too, so the pressure's not all on you. But she'll probably be too busy having drunk sex."

He widened his eyes.

"I'm sorry," I said. "That came out of nowhere. It's just—"

"Don't worry about it," Mike said. "What am I going to do, go tell her you said that?"

"You're going to go have drunk bar sex with her."

"All right," Mike said, opening the front door. "Yes, I promise I'll keep in touch. But only because we weirdos need to stick together." If Mike was a weirdo, I didn't know what I was. A freak of nature.

"Well, see you," he said, putting up a fist. I bumped it.

"Not if I see you first."

"I don't even know what that saying means."

"Me either."

I drove the five minutes home in silence. I felt more real after seeing Mike. I also felt lonelier than I had in a while. But at least I had something to tell Jane.


By my next appointment, the weather had turned freezing and slushy—my jeans were already stained with salt and I'd only gone from the house to the garage to the car to the office building—yet Jane looked pristine in a cream sweater, green tweed skirt, and shiny black stiletto boots. Maybe she changed at the office. If I ever chose to dress to impress, I'd have to ask her her secrets.

"Hey, it looks better in here," I said when I entered her office, which now was painted a warmer taupe color and carpeted in navy.

"Yeah—the carpet's that crappy industrial stuff but still better than hearing my voice echo in here. So what's new with you?"

"So I guess I'm losing Kate," I said. "I don't know. I feel really sad when I hear a song that we used to sing together or remember some stupid joke that made us laugh until our stomachs hurt. I doubt we'll ever be that close again."

"Well, you don't know," said Jane. "A lot of people grow apart at first and then get back in touch once they've settled down and figured out who they are at college."

"Kate hasn't had a problem figuring out who she is," I said.

"Why do you think that?"

"I don't know. She doesn't sound like it. She sounds like she's having a lot of fun, and she's really popular, and she's, like, drinking and being *totally cool.*" I started getting really sarcastic in the second half of that sentence. "And she fucks everything that moves," I said.

"Whoa."

"Okay, I didn't mean to say it like that," I said. "She's having a lot of sex, I guess, or so she tells me. I guess that's what you do in college. That's fine. I can admit I'm sort of inexperienced or prudish, so maybe I'm jealous. But it's like—she seems to think it's making her cool. And she was . . . already cool before. It makes me sad."

"Maybe she's just not meant to be your friend anymore," she said.

"She outgrew me."

"Who says?" Jane said. "Just because she's in college? Or she let a guy put his penis in her vagina? That doesn't automatically mean she got more mature than you."

I shrugged.

Jane smiled. "Did you consider that maybe she's not that cool if she's leaving you behind in the dust?" she said. "Maybe she actually kind of sucks."

"Well, still. I'm not wearing a sombrero and having people drink tequila out of my belly button," I said. "Nobody's drinking anything out of my belly button. But you know what, I don't blame her. I feel like I forfeited the right to have friends or something."

"How so?"

"I don't know . . . why should I expect my friends to take their precious college time to talk to me, to pity me just because I couldn't move on somehow?"

"What about your friend Mike?"

"Mike's a nice guy. Everyone likes him."

"But if everyone likes him, wouldn't that mean he'd also be too busy to talk to you?"

"Maybe he just wants to talk to me because I make him feel better about himself—like maybe he might have transferred from a really good school just to be with a chick, but at least he's in school. Talking to me makes him feel better."

"Why would you bother talking to someone who just pities you, then?"

"I don't know," I said.

"Have you and Mike ever hooked up?" Jane asked. I snorted. "Why is that so funny? Are you guys not saying 'hooked up' anymore?"

"No," I said. "We just don't have that kind of relationship. He dates other girls. I'm his pal. I wouldn't want to make things weird. Even if I *could* make things weird, which I wouldn't. I haven't even tried."

"You don't want to go there," she said. I rolled my eyes. "People don't say 'go there' anymore? I'm the youngest person in this office, but I feel so old when I talk to patients like you."

"Sorry," I said. "No, I haven't wanted to 'go there.'"

"Hmm, okay, so maybe you didn't go there with Mike—what about other guys?"

But the truth was, overall, I hadn't even really thought about guys very much since coming back from my day at college. It was hard to feel seductive or cute or just not ridiculous when you lived at home with your dad because you ran away from school. It was easy to ignore the fact that I had no romance in my life so far. There was very little to remind me of such things until I did see Mike and I was suddenly reminded of said things, and it reminded me how much nicer it was to pretend these things didn't exist.

My experience with guys was pretty limited at this point. And, by and large, I didn't mind it: the guys in high school didn't impress me too much, and typically they didn't seem to be worth breaking up a friendship over, which is what they typically seemed to do. The only experience I had to speak of was the summer between sophomore year and junior year of high school, when Kate and I were assistant counselors at a sleepaway camp in Michigan. My campers loathed me, and I hated them right back. They were spiteful, bitter little sixth graders who had hoped for a counselor who would help them curl their hair and make bead bracelets as opposed to rolling her eyes throughout their talent-show practices and refusing to buy them candy on her night out. One of the only things I really liked about camp was that it was totally acceptable to do things like quit shaving your legs and stop wearing makeup. I took advantage of this by going as long as I could without washing my hair, which I kept in a permanent set of braids.

Camp was more stressful in some ways than school, because everybody matched up and hooked up, despite the greasy hair and mosquito-bitten legs. Kate found Joe, a freakishly tall and thin fellow with long blond hair who was actually from Michigan (ooh la la). The two of them would hold hands and quietly disappear into the woods together. In those days, she didn't feel the need to report every detail of her love life, plus there was only one guy to keep track of.

I can't remember if I just decided to have a crush on Ethan or if I actually did have a crush on him. He was a year older than us. He was certainly all right enough, but sort of B-class material, the guy who would hang back and laugh as his friends performed silly antics. He was pretty cute, with a thatch of overgrown reddish hair and big dark brown eyes. We had nothing to talk about, but after dark, when the counselors slipped out of the cabin to our "staff meetings" and all made out or smoked pot, Ethan and I would sit together on the field along with the other counselors who weren't screwing or smoking. He gave me awful back rubs, soft and ineffective, but it was still nice to have someone touching my back, even if it was in a lackluster manner.

"You liiiike him," Kate said after the first night the two of us hung out, walking back to our cement-floored cabins.

"Shut up."

"Laaaaaaaah," she said. She was just excited because she let Joe touch her boob that night.

"He *is* cute," I admitted, begrudgingly.

"What do you guys talk about?" she asked. "Cuteness and liking each other?"

"Oh good god, I could never talk to him!" I couldn't. It felt really embarrassing for some reason. Just sitting next to each other and being cuddly felt okay, though.

"CECILY HAS A BOYFRIEND!" the sixth-grade girls all sang when I tried to open the screen door to the cabin without making a sound.

"You little slags better shut up," I hissed, and went to my bunk, excited and terrified about seeing Ethan the next day. The senior counselor had put on a Coldplay album to listen to while she fell asleep, and for the first time it sounded kind of romantic and not just bland.

We were both too shy to really do anything except maybe put our heads on each other's shoulders, but on the night before we were due to go home, he asked if I wanted to go for a walk.

"Okay," I said, and my heart started beating hard, because obviously this was the point where I was going to have sex and have a baby. Actually, we'd probably just kiss, but the obviousness of it, the soon-it-will-be-time-to-kiss-ness of it gave me plenty of opportunity to get nervous.

Did we talk? We probably did. About what, who knows? Bug spray? The shittiness of my kids? How we'd be going home soon? I don't remember. I just remember how romantic it was down by the lake. It was about midnight, but something, probably the moon reflecting off the clouds, made it seem almost light out. Crickets chirped. Water lapped. I wanted to puke. I mean, not only from nervousness; it was so cliché, I almost couldn't stand it.

We faced each other. Ethan chuckled and plucked at one of my braids. Then we kissed and I was so nervous, my hands were shaking. He was probably a decent kisser in that I don't remember being grossed out or anything, but I didn't have time to notice. I was just trying to act like I wasn't freaking out, which of course made me seem completely nervous.

"Relax," he whispered. What did he look like in the dark? Was he smiling? Did he look serious? I couldn't tell. All I remember was his smell: a musty smell of dust and sweat that would probably smell repellent in everyday situations, but was oddly comforting at camp.

It didn't last long. I heard someone calling my name and scrambled back to the campground. One of my kids, probably just to spite me, decided that she was going to get homesick the night before it was time to go home. But I was actually grateful. I wouldn't have known what to do next.

Ethan was going to ride back to his suburb (thankfully, we didn't go to the same school) with a friend, and I was stuck with bus duty. Before he headed back to his cabin to collect his stuff, he came to meet me by the giant huffing buses that would take everyone back home. We sheepishly grinned at each other. We clearly didn't know what to do. Were we boyfriend and girlfriend now? Would we never speak again? I decided to do what I had done all summer and leaned my head on his shoulder, and he wrapped his arms around me as obnoxious kids tapped on the windows of the bus above us. I couldn't wait to get going.

Ethan pressed a folded-up scrap of notebook paper in my hand. It was too small to say anything meaningful: it was almost certainly his phone number. I couldn't handle the responsibility of calling a boy, having to talk to him, having to get to know him as a regular in-school guy, not a camp counselor. On the ride home, as the big black garbage bag got passed up toward the aisle for kids to dispose of the remains of their boxed lunches, I put the number inside and felt relieved as it slipped between apple cores, banana peels, sandwich crusts, and granola bar wrappers—beyond my realm of responsibility.

That next summer, I asked my dad if there were any jobs for me at his university, and I spent it blissfully but boringly filing in the history department office, far away from Ethan and the possibility of kissing.


"So," I said after telling this to Jane.

"So," she said. "I guess you're seeing one of the downsides of staying behind while everyone moves on."

That stung. "Yeah," I said. "Yeah, I guess I am." She looked at me, and I couldn't tell if the expression on her face said,

"Well, what are you going to do now?" Or, "You poor thing." Or maybe it said, "I'm hungry." I didn't feel like trying to figure out what it meant, and anyway, the appointment was over. "Well, see you, Jane," I said.

Dad picked me up from my appointment.

"How was it?" he asked.

"Fine," I said, and looked out the window at a Starbucks across the street. Kids from the university were curled up inside, studying in pairs. I felt pathetic.

"Want to talk about it?" he asked, turning left toward the lake.

"NO," I nearly shouted. When we got home, I made a beeline to my room and tried to whip up some tears to make myself feel better, first because I was a pathetic, lonely person not doing something with my life. Second, because I was a bad daughter. But nothing came of it.

# february

**I had strong opinions** on daytime television. *Oprah* was always good as long as it wasn't about self-improvement. Shows with more than one host were usually awful unless a guest host was sitting in. I liked Judge Mathis because he reminded me of one of my favorite teachers from grade school. But while I was a merciless critic, that didn't mean I didn't watch it all. I tried to do it on the sly, though: when Dad was out of the house, because I knew he'd get pissed if he caught me lounging on the couch watching yet another teenager screaming at an audience, "Fuck you! Y'all don't know me!"

Unfortunately, Dad came home for an early lunch one day when I was watching an episode of *Jerry Springer* that involved very fat men who enjoyed eating sloppily while not wearing many clothes.

"Oh, hi, Dad," I said, trying to keep my cool as I hastily turned off the TV.

"Nice way to spend your day," he said.

"I was just about to take Superhero for a walk," I said. Superhero, who had been lying on the floor next to me, raised his head at the *w* word. Fortunately, he couldn't speak and tell Dad he'd already been on one.

"Okay," said Dad. "I just came up here to let you know that I took the liberty of setting up a meeting with a professional."

"What? No."

"Yes."

"NO."

"YES."

"Let me just get this straight before we keep going," I said. "A professional what? I'm already seeing a professional therapist."

"A professional college counselor," said Dad. "I never trusted those counselors at your high school anyway. There weren't enough of them, and they knew nothing about you."

This was true. My school supplied four counselors to seven hundred kids in my graduating class. Mine was named Robin, and I never even found out for myself if Robin was a man or a woman. But it could have been worse: there was one girl in our class named Hillary Thomas who was applying to Brown, who got rejected because her counselor accidentally sent them the transcript of a girl named Heather Thompson. Heather had dropped out early in the year to have a baby. In the end, Hillary got in anyway, which was good because Hillary was a superintense overachiever and many people, I won't name names, found it amusing when her head nearly exploded after not getting into Brown.

But still. I didn't want to see a counselor. Kate's parents had hired one. Her name was Claudia Something-or-other but Kate referred to her as the Claw. Kate's parents paid thousands of dollars for her to sit in a room with the Claw, apparently a dried-out husk of a woman who wore "whimsical" jewelry decorated with little wooden animals. They would make lists of possible schools Kate could attend, based on Kate's personality. The Claw then encouraged Kate to join the basketball team, build a house with Habitat for Humanity, and join a church youth group, all within the last four months of school, to pump up her application. Kate knew before she even saw the Claw where she wanted to go, but her parents basically just wanted to see if maybe there was some way the Claw could convince Kate to apply to Princeton and just maybe Kate would get in, and then just maybe her parents could mention to all their friends, casually, that they had a daughter who went to Princeton. Unfortunately for them, Kate did not get into Princeton, because, unbeknownst to them, she blew off the interview to go get ice cream sundaes with me. Kate would repeat to me in the Claw's husky voice, "You know, if you're *really* serious about this, you would . . ."

It all sounded completely unhelpful, annoying, and a lot of bullshit, and I was through with that part of applying to colleges—the making-yourself-look-better-than-you-are part.

"I don't want to," I said.

"Too bad," Dad said. "You have an appointment with her next week. Someone at work recommended her. They said she's great. Speaking of which, you know, I can always speak to the dean and you can go to college right here in town. You could still live at home."

"*No.*" I would not be a pity case who ended up going to the school where her father worked. I would not go to college less than a mile away from my house. I probably wouldn't get in anyway.

"Cecily, what do you want? I'm at the end of my rope here. I'm trying to help you."

"I don't know, what *SHOULD* I want?"

"You should want whatever makes you happy."

"Well, I don't fucking know what that is yet. Tell me what to do."

He opened his mouth to say something, closed it, and took a breath. "I *am* telling you what to do, and that's to see the counselor—at least to see if she helps. And when you do meet with her you'd better have some thought of what you're looking or not looking for."

"Well, I'm not the same as I once was, you know. Things change," I said, trying to sound world-weary and knowledge-able.

"Apparently, they do, because you were sorta easy to deal with a few months ago and now you're a total—"

"I think I want something where I can just have a lot of opportunities to figure out what I want," I said.

Dad beamed. "See? That wasn't so hard."

I was so full of crap. I realized something, though. Dad was thinking, or maybe hoping, that the college was the problem, the reason I turned around the year before. And that all I needed was a better school to keep me there. That was interesting.

• • •

**february**

I was in a foul mood the day of my appointment. Dad dropped me off (the same building as Dr. Stern), which meant I had to walk home. It would probably be a twenty-minute walk and it was a mild day, but I hated having exercise forced on me. Plus, I hated my outfit. At the last minute I had picked a long-sleeved T-shirt and down-filled vest to wear with my jeans, but the wind still blew off the lake pretty strongly and I knew I'd be freezing on my long journey home. This seemed like a real intrusion upon my precious time, too. If there was one thing I knew I was totally over, it was the college application and selection process. God, it was a drag. Repeating everything you've done, trying to convince people how special you are. Reading back through the college books hadn't made me feel any more nostalgic for it. This was going to suck.

"Hi!" said a perky girl with blond hair as I entered the office, this one on the fourth floor.

"Hi," I said. "I'm Cecily Powell."

"Great," she said, clicking a few things on her computer. "Okay, it looks like you have a noon with Leah. You're going to love her. She's the best."

"Great," I said.

"She'll be right with you."

"Fine."

The girl put some headphones in and started humming as I flopped onto one of the sleek black leather couches. Sunlight streamed into the office, but that didn't help the hideous reading material selection. *U.S. News & World Report* and the same college books I had at home. There were a few framed letters on the wall. I glanced at them but quit paying attention after I read, "Dear Leah!!! Oh my God. I am loving it at Dartmouth."

Dear Whoever. Shut up. I hate you.

Aargh. I had a horrible feeling that it was so *obvious* that I didn't belong in this office, that it wasn't going to help me at all. But I couldn't come up with a good reason why. And in the meantime I was stuck, because Dad definitely was going to give me a quiz if I came out of here without sounding like I had gotten something out of it—he had promised before he dropped me off. Dad wasn't much of a disciplinarian, but he was serious when he told us to pay attention to things. When we went on trips, he would refuse to buy us souvenirs unless we could speak for at least five minutes on what we had seen.

"Hey, hi, hi," said a woman rushing in through the reception room door, carrying some files and a plastic shopping bag. At least two purses hung from her shoulders, plus a backpack. She was wearing one of those long black superpuffy coats that a lot of people wear in Chicago in the winter. It basically looks like a comforter with sleeves. I'm sure they're very cozy, but I just couldn't bring myself to buy or wear one, ever. For the coldest days, I had convinced my dad to buy me a bright red and black North Face jacket, which, he informed me, cost enough that I would never need another winter coat for as long as I lived—so I was stuck with mine anyway. She had long, frizzy-curly black hair that was being crowded out by a lot of white. It was probably what mine would look like when I was a crazy old lady myself one day. She shuffled through the lobby and through the door separating the office from the reception area. The door slammed behind her. Less than a minute later, the perky girl at the front desk pulled out one of her headphones and picked up the ringing phone. She hung up and said, "Okay, Cecily! Leah is ready for you. Just head through this door. Hers is the office to the right."

"Thanks," I said, and trudged through the door.

Leah was definitely the crazy-looking lady with the frizzy hair. She was still taking off her coat when I walked into her office. Her window offered a nice view of an unusual apartment building across the street. For some reason, the architects had designed it with this funny top to it that made it look German, vaguely like a gingerbread house. I could see a little strip of blue lake on the horizon.

"Hi, Cecily. It is Cecily, right? Unless you go by any nick-names?"

"Nope," I said, and then wished I had said something like, "Why, actually, most of my friends call me 'Moon Unit'" to see if she would play along.

"Have a seat," she said, gesturing to the chair on the other side of her desk. "You don't mind if I eat, do you?" Actually, I did mind. I was starving, and her Jimmy John's sandwich looked amazing. It made me hate this all the more. Dad had woken me up at eleven-thirty for my noon appointment, which gave me exactly fifteen minutes to get up and go. I used those fifteen minutes to shower, not eat breakfast. I started to complain about how hungry I was as he drove, but he shot me a look that made me shut up.

"It's fine." I shrugged. Her office was decorated with post-ers of university campuses and more letters, presumably from satisfied customers.

"Okay," she said. "Apologies in advance if I spill all over myself and/or have onion breath."

I gave a fake half smile.

"So, Cecily," she said, licking some mayonnaise off her fingers and then flipping through a few pages in a file that she apparently already had on me. "What can I help you with today?"

"I don't know, really," I said. "My dad signed me up for this and didn't really tell me."

"Believe it or not, I hear that a lot," she said.

"Yeah," I said. It came out as more of a statement than a question. A conversation-ender.

"Hmm." She obviously had wanted me to ask, "Oh really?" or something, but I wasn't in the mood to chitchat. "Well, do you have any idea why you're here?"

I didn't know if she was playing some sort of psych game or if she just didn't know what was up. "You don't know yet, really? Or are you asking me, like, so I can figure out out loud what I should be thinking about?"

"Sure," she said. "Whatever." She opened a bag of potato chips. They smelled delicious. Krunchers! They were always great, despite their corny name. "Tell me why you think you're here. It shouldn't matter either way if I know or not, because your answer should be the same, right?" she asked. Ugh.

"Well, okay. I'm taking the year off."

"Why?"

"It just wasn't time yet."

"Time for what?" she said, munching. Damn her and those chips.

"Time for, you know, school. I went to start my freshman year, but I couldn't do it. I turned around and went home."

Leah looked me straight in the eye over her long nose as she sipped from her takeout cup. She kind of looked like an owl. She put it down on the desk, hard, and made that *Aaah* noise you make after you're particularly refreshed.

"Okay. Let's try this. What do you think you want from a college?" Leah asked.

"I don't know," I said, staring at the desk.

"You seem fairly bright," she said, glancing at my file. "So whatever your particular issue is that compelled you not to go through with your year, I'm assuming it's not an academic thing. Or a drug problem or anything like that."

I just stared out the window at the weird German-looking building.

"Okay, Cecily," Leah said, leaning back in her chair. She let her head slouch to her shoulder and looked out the window at the German building, not at me. "I can respect that it maybe wasn't your choice to be here and that you're questioning the point of this. But seriously? I'm getting a little fucking sick of the attitude. Don't you think you're a little too old for this?" I blinked, hard, and I started feeling funny in my stomach. My heart began racing.

"Now," she said. "I know you didn't come here because you don't care about wasting your dad's money. And I know you're not acting like this because you're a spoiled brat." She looked at me expectantly, but smiling.

"Um. No."

"Good," she said. "Because I don't want to have to kick you out of here. I hate kicking people out of here. But I really hate it when my time is wasted. I've spent too much precious time on snotty kids, and believe me, there are a lot of them in this town."

I snorted out a gross-sounding laugh. She laughed, too.

"It's okay," she said. "We can both admit it. But that's all right. At least it's just you," she said. "Sometimes I get to see these kids' parents yell at them in front of me. Or they answer for their kids like it's a ventriloquist act. Or I start questioning the kids' attitude and then their parents question *my* attitude and I have to kick them all out and then have a good cry."

"I think my dad wants me to figure it out on my own," I said. "I guess he thinks he can't figure this all out for me. He was a lot pushier with my sister when she was my age, and she didn't turn out much better than me. I think she's worse."

"Helicopter parents are not always the best," Leah said, and I imagined for a minute what it would be like if Dad *had* made me apply to more schools, tougher schools, had made me take the SATs two or three times, had rung up his colleagues for recommendations. Would I be better off? We probably wouldn't get along as well, that's for sure.

"So what's up, Cecily?" she said, looking me in the eye again and leaning forward in her chair. The way she said it made me think she knew exactly what my situation was. For a second, I wanted to cry.

"I don't know," I said. "I don't know what's up."

"So you picked Kenyon, huh?" she said, flipping some more through my file. "It's a good school. I have a lot of friends from there. You can talk to some of them if you want.

They all loved it there. I can't say that for everybody I know who went to other schools."

Kenyon. I liked it because the name sounded like "canyon." And because they sent me a cool-looking brochure that featured a leaf-strewn path with friends enjoying soon-to-be precious college memories together. And also because I got in there. As I told Leah, Dad had pushed Germaine pretty hard when it came to picking out colleges. Josh was a goody-goody who graduated in the top quarter of the class, so he pushed himself. I didn't know if Dad was tired from pushing Germaine, hoped I'd be like Josh, or what, but while he checked in to make sure that I was actually remembering to look at schools and apply to them, and recommended some he thought I might like (all small liberal arts schools), he seemed satisfied as long as I was applying to places that had a semidecent reputation and weren't too far away and didn't cost an arm and a leg to go to. I received the brochure for Kenyon, applied, and got in. I didn't have a big plan for what would happen once I got there, what I'd major in or join or whatever. I was okay at everything. Probably less capable at math and science. I liked Spanish. I just figured I'd start college and by the end figure out what I was going to do.

I mostly liked the school because it didn't look too much like anything. Josh's school definitely had a frat and party atmosphere. It was a good university, but it wasn't like kids were going to museums with their free time or anything. Germaine went to a small college that was 89 percent women, and I was convinced that the smallness and womanliness of it were partially what made her crazy. We fought before she left for college, but I thought that we'd get along better after she came back. I was wrong, though: I think she got so used to fighting with girls for four years that she was just going to keep going. Also, I think that was why she was boy crazy and lazy. After four years of being told the importance of being a strong woman, a leading woman, Germaine just didn't want to do anything.

Kate's college was prestigious but hippie-ish, the kind where most of the kids were filthy and stunk like incense and shopped at co-ops, but were also all really rich. Everyone at Mike's former school seemed like assholes. I had no real basis for this stereotype, but I was going to go with it. I had no idea what the University of Kansas was like, other than the fact that it was located in Kansas.

I liked Kenyon because it seemed like I didn't have to join a club, be an asshole, or be too smart or too independent or too womanly or too girly or live in Kansas. And now I liked it because I could go there without having to send in an application.

As I talked to Leah, I figured out what it was about her that seemed odd. She was about my dad's age, maybe ten years younger, but the way she listened to me and said "Uh-huh," or "Oh really?" or "like" instead of "said" and really looked at me while I talked, it was more like a friend, or someone my age. I didn't know what to think. Germaine and I never had conversations on purpose, and my mother never seemed to listen to me that closely when I talked. I wasn't sure if I liked Leah, but I liked talking to her. It felt like one of the few normal conversations I'd had all year. I wondered if she was a mom. I didn't see a wedding band on, but I saw some picture frames on her desk, though I couldn't see what was in them. They could have contained babies, or a sailboat, or dogs. I wondered what it would be like to have a mom like her. She seemed cool with her own dorkiness.

"Okay," she said when I was done talking about where I might have gone to school. "Let's start from the beginning, though, and get a few other options in there. What size student body were you looking for?"

"Seriously?" I said. "In all seriousness, I don't think it's the school. I was ready to go to Kenyon. And then it went to shit."

"Well, you know it's also my job to help kids figure out if college just isn't right for them," she said. "I've had plenty of kids go into the army, or they went right to work, or they traveled first."

"I don't want to join the army," I said. "I would suck at being in the army."

"Do you think there's something about a university setting that just isn't right for you?" she asked. "You could always take classes online."

I made a face, and she snorted. She took a huge plate-size cookie out of her fast-food bag, unwrapped it, and held it out for me to break off a piece. I declined. I didn't believe in sharing desserts. When I went in, I went in all the way.

"No," I said. "That sounds superboring."

"That's good," she said, some cookie bits falling onto her chunky gray sweater. "We're establishing that you're not totally socially inept."

"I am, kind of."

"That's okay. Me too. I mean, *obviously*," she said, looking down at the crumbs on her sweater. We sat in silence for a few moments. The room was quiet except for a few whooshes from cars down the street below.

"You know what," I said, "I know I shouldn't take it for granted, but I always just assumed I'd go to college. I know there are kids in the world who would love to but they can't afford it, but I just assumed I'd go anyway. I didn't worry about going. My dad always talked about me going the way he had talked about my brother and sister going, and they went. I took it for granted that it would happen."

"You're lucky."

"Yeah."

"So you're thinking that assumption was wrong?"

"No," I said. "Because I think not going, ever, would feel weirder than going. Despite all the issues I apparently have with it."

"What are the issues?"

"I don't know," I said. "Like, everyone ends up the same when they go to college. It's all about partying and awesomeness and getting drunk and going to class." Based on my conversations with Kate, anyway.

"Well," she said, "that's not entirely inaccurate."

"And," I said, "I don't even know if I would have any friends anyway. I'm hardly friends anymore with the people I went to high school with, and I've known them for years. And everyone's going to think I'm a freak when they find out I'm older than them."

"Well, they won't. But you're obviously afraid of blending in too much, losing your identity."

"Right."

"But I also get the feeling that you're afraid of not having any friends at all."

"I guess that's right."

"Well, Cecily, I gotta tell you," Leah said, wadding up the cellophane from the cookie into a ball. "I know it's my job to help you find which schools would make you happiest and be best for you, and then try to help you get in there. But, like you said, it doesn't sound like it's the school that's the issue. I mean, yes, I think you actually would be better off at Kenyon than, say, University of Arizona. But all that other stuff—that's up to you. I actually think it's pretty cool that you're doing your own thing, even if you don't know why you're doing it. All these parents *shove* their kids into the system, and nobody really seems to know why. They have an idea that it's going to be helpful down the road somehow. That if they don't power through and go-go-go, then they're going to be fucked for life. You *should* question it. I question it and it's my job, for Christ's sake."

"Well, I don't know if I'm questioning *it* or *me* or what," I said. I liked the idea that I was actually a rebel, fighting The Man and not letting myself be led through the cattle chute of my late teens. But I didn't mind The Man. I was probably afraid of The Man more than anything else. I didn't want to fight him.

"Cecily?" she said. "My advice? Don't worry so much."

"Aren't you paid to get me to worry about it?"

"No," she said. "I don't get kickbacks from schools for sending them there. I'll get your money regardless of whether you go to college or go get pregnant and have six kids and move to Peoria."

"What?"

"Our hour is up," she said sweetly. "Come back and see me if you want. Or don't."

"Okay," I said. I did sort of want to come back and see her again, just to talk to her, not even to help with college stuff. Maybe in some alternate universe.

"Okay," she said.

I got up and put my vest on. "Good luck," she said as I opened the door.

"You too," I said. I had closed the door before I realized that I meant to say, "Thanks," because I wasn't wishing her luck on anything, but I let it go.

The walk home wasn't nearly as bad as I had dreaded; in fact, it felt good to actually move around. I bought a hot chocolate on the way, which, of course, made the entire world more pleasant. Except for Germaine, who was in the kitchen when I got home, heating up a Lean Cuisine and basically making the entire kitchen reek.

"How was Leah?" she asked.

"Fine," I said suspiciously. I didn't know Germaine was so in on my plans.

"I saw her once, you know," she said. "She didn't help me at all. I think she's an idiot."

"Well, I kind of liked her," I said. She snorted and took out her dish of sadness, stirred it, and put it back in the micro-wave.

"So? What did she say?" she asked.

"Oh, you know . . ." I said, hoping to make that profound

statement last until I could find Superhero's leash and get back out of the house. This was unpleasant.

"No, I *don't* know," Germaine said. "I'm just curious about what she told you."

"Why?" I asked. "Why should it matter to you?"

"Everybody just wants to know why, Cecily. That's really it. Once we know why, then we can just go back to ignoring you and let you have your little year off."

I rolled my eyes. "Well, I don't know why, so fuck off." The only thing that really bothered me was the way she said "everybody," like everybody was gathering together to whisper about me. But of course, to her, that was what I wanted.

"Oh, come on," said Germaine. "You can't have been that scared. It's not like you haven't gone away before. You're not completely socially inept. You're not fat. Are you crazy? Or are you just acting crazy because you want attention?"

"Yes," I said. "That's exactly it. And oh how I enjoy this. I'm really having fun with the attention I'm getting right now."

"I bet you are," she said.

"You know, contrary to what you might think, I didn't orchestrate this just to piss you off," I said. "I didn't really think this through at all. Okay? I did something and I clearly didn't have a follow-up plan. But I'll tell you this: if I knew it would be this much fun, I probably wouldn't have done it."

# march

**"I want you to get a job,"** said Jane at our next appointment. This was possibly a good idea, as I was starting to get cabin fever as most people in Chicago did. Even though the rest of the country was apparently undergoing something called "spring," here it was still winter. Still, going to work wasn't really my idea of what to do on spring break.

"Ah," I said. "Believe it or not, I don't really need a lot of spending money. I'm actually saving money, when you think of it."

"That's nice. It's not really so much about you earning cash. It's about direction."

"Well, actually, I met with a college counselor—"

"You did?"

"Yeah, and we agreed that I probably should go back to school anyway."

"Well, first of all, I think that's great that you met with a counselor," said Jane, who looked so legitimately happy it was weird. "Was it helpful?"

"Um, yes and no. I'm probably just going to try to go back to Kenyon. I still think it's the school for me. We'll just see if it's the year for me."

"Cecily, that's great! You have a plan, at least. That's a big step."

"Oh stop. You're much too kind," I said with pretend modesty, although I did feel embarrassed all of a sudden. I felt like I was being congratulated for getting a C on a test, or maybe just putting my socks on right-side-out.

"Well, anyway, you clearly still need to get out of the house and occupy yourself. And, yes, get a little spending money. Go out and have fun."

"I'm not a big shopper," I said. "Maybe you could take me."

Jane ignored me. "Your dad works at the university, right? Maybe he can get you something?" She pulled out a piece of paper and began scrawling.

Actually, it wasn't unheard of for me to go help my dad out with filing from time to time (like when I wanted to escape having to see people). I didn't exactly love it, but there was something pleasant about hanging out in the offices.

"I guess, yeah."

"And you'll at least be around some people your age. Ooh! In fact, maybe you can sit in on a class or two."

"Okay, Jane. Let's not get crazy. Maybe I don't want to be around people my age. Maybe I should just work in a geriatric home or something. All the old people I know seem to take a shine to me—Dad, you . . ."

"You're very funny, you know that?" Jane said, and handed me the paper, which read, "Rx: Work!"

Ugh. For the first time I wished I *was* taking a fancy year off, because I bet I could be in Greece right now or something, getting swarthy and eating flaming cheese instead of agreeing to get a job *and* go to class. Greece definitely sounded more fun.

"Good-bye, Cecily."

Gina was wearing headphones when I came out, listening to music so loud I could hear it from several feet away. I pounded on the countertop, just once, hard, with my fist, and fled before I could see her look up.


At home, Dad and I got into a stupid fight about me going to work with him. To summarize, it went something like this:

"Jane the Shrink says to ask if I can work with you a few days a week or something. I need structure and to get out of the house and to socialize."

"Good, because I was going to tell you that you needed to find a job anyway."

"Oh, you were going to *tell* me this? You were going to *make* me?" Suddenly the idea of working for my dad, which was only mildly annoying before, now seemed completely unfair.

"Yes."

"What if I didn't want to work? What if I wanted to travel?"

"Well, *do* you want to travel?"

"No."

"Sometimes I don't get you, Cecily."

I shrugged. "I'm an enigma!"

He shook his head. "Don't be cute. Here's the deal. I'm not going to fund your year of sitting around doing nothing anymore. You're coming to work with me on Monday. End of story."

"Fine!" I said, and ran outside with Superhero to try to calm down and figure out what I was upset about anyway. Dad and I hadn't been getting along so great lately, and it was making me feel guilty. Either I was clearly bugging him for, I think, not knowing what I was going to do with myself, or he was irritating me with his attempts to help me. I guessed he was being helpful, but I didn't want it.

It didn't help that by this time Germaine had found a job, too, one downtown doing some assistant work at a law firm. I don't think she was happy with it at all: she came home every day crabby from the commute and from doing boring work, but despite her irritability, she seemed to get along better with Dad, who was nicer to her now that she wasn't just lying around all the time. I didn't mind the concept of working when it was my own idea, but I didn't like it when it sounded mandatory. Plus, shouldn't I try to find a job somewhere other than Dad's university? I already knew that place. I was used to the vision of kids in backpacks crossing long paths on their way to class, the fliers taped to the ground advertising sit-ins or walkouts or dance marathons. I had been in the huge, scary library where everyone seemed strange and serious. I had seen the tour groups, wide-eyed or sullen kids and their parents being led around by some jerkoff prep kid walking backward, explaining excitedly how old the old clock tower was and the differences between the various a cappella singing groups on campus.

Dad would be farming me out for odd jobs around the department offices for a few days each week. To start off, I'd be filing for him. He had implemented a new filing system, finally, but he didn't want to inflict the pain of reorganizing everything on his personal assistant, Sue, so he was going to inflict it on me for ten dollars an hour.

We drove to his office. Dad showed me how the new system would work, and I sat on my butt on the floor, reorganizing in the history department's cozy reception area. I worked like this, in silence, for three hours. I didn't mind it, really. I liked organizing things. It brought hope to whatever I was working on at that moment, like everything would be new and clean and ready for the future. Every once in a while, Hugo, the snippy receptionist, would clear his throat in a way that seemed like he was hinting at something, but I'd look up and he'd still be looking at the computer. Hugo always pretended not to know who I was anytime I came by to visit or called Dad's office. For some reason, he seemed like he hated me, and that was fine. It probably would be a lot more boring in the office without someone to hate.

"Cecily," Dad said, popping his head out eventually, "I have some meetings at lunchtime, so I can't eat with you. Is that okay?"

"Fine," I said. "I understand you don't want me to cramp your style."

"Here's some money," he said. "You know where the food court is, right? Hugo can show you."

"I know where it is," I said. I didn't want to have to make small talk with Hugo, and I'm sure he felt the same way.

A chilly wind was blowing off the lake, making campus inhospitable, so I decided to avoid the food court and walk to Kafein, a dark and cozy café a few blocks away, where I could hide in a booth.

"'Scuse me," said a girl walking past me on a cobblestone path that was typically shaded by trees in the summer. She looked about Germaine's age, maybe a little older. "Do you know where Kedzie Hall is?"

"Sorry," I said. "I don't go here."

"Oh," she said, looking annoyed. "Thanks." I couldn't really blame her for being annoyed. I probably looked like I went there. Otherwise, why would I just be running around on campus, unleashed?

At lunch, I had a tuna salad sandwich on a pita and some potato chips and read one of the many free weekly papers that were spread carelessly throughout the coffee shop. Life in the city. It was sort of a mystery to me. Of course, we went into town all the time for dinner or plays or museum exhibits or baseball games, but we always came back home. Growing up and moving into a high-rise, walking to the grocery store, taking the bus a few blocks to listen to a concert? It seemed as attainable to me as becoming a professional skier.

I took a hot chocolate to go, walked back, and sat on one of the many cold marble benches that were scattered around campus—they all had dates stamped in the stone, for the class that had donated them. You'd think an entire class could afford to donate more than just a bench, but maybe they were more expensive than they looked. I felt like a spy, blending in with these other kids. I played a game—could I see myself among these students? Was I one of them, just waiting to bloom? Or was I really just not cut out for college? My hypothesis was that I'd find 75 percent of the people who left or entered the building repellent in some way.

At first I was pleased. A bunch of girls exited a dorm looking like the Louis Vuitton Mafia: they all wore expensive winter ski coats and carried big purses on their arms and sported jeans that I recognized from Germaine's closet as costing close to two hundred dollars a pair. They seemed to be giggling about something, probably guys. And, as they passed by me, I saw their eyes glance over me, just quickly enough to know that they were evaluating me somehow. To be honest, I would have thought they were bitches even if they hadn't looked at me.

But then classes must have let out, because dozens of kids suddenly came pouring out of the nearby classroom buildings. I saw all different kinds of people at once—nerds, athletes, weirdos, but mostly people who I couldn't really categorize, people in jeans and backpacks and gym shoes. I got cold, and the game grew boring.


Dad also liked Jane's idea of me taking a class, so he arranged for me to audit an introduction to art history. It was a lecture, so I wouldn't have to participate and I wouldn't have to take the final or even do homework if I didn't want to.

"What's the point, then?" I asked when he told me on the

drive home from campus, and I instantly regretted it, because I already knew what he'd say.

"Are you really asking me this question?" he said. "This is what I do for a living. What's the point? Oh, I don't know, how about *to learn*?" he said, his voice rising. "To sit around with people your own age and do what people your age do? Or maybe I'm just trying to torture you."

"You're right, I'm sorry," I said.

He was quiet for a second. "If you really don't want to do this, then don't, Cecily," Dad said. "But I'm trying to help you. I'm not really sure how to help you right now, so you either need to give me input or just give me a break."

"Okay," I said. "Don't worry about it. I'll go." I couldn't really explain to him that I was terrified about going and sitting in a classroom with a bunch of other kids for some reason. Walking by them on campus, even sitting by them in the cafeteria, was a strange but usually tolerable experience. But sitting with them in a lecture hall for an hour, I'd be trapped. They'd immediately pick me out as a poseur the second I opened my mouth.

I didn't know what to expect, really. I had liked the art history classes I had taken in high school, but I didn't know what to expect from a college course. I wasn't sure my brain would be up for any challenge.

The first day of class, I woke up with that first-day-of-school feeling, which made me feel immediately embarrassed, and then I felt embarrassed for feeling embarrassed in my own bedroom. Since I'd started working, I had to dress a little more presentably—not anything very formal, but sweaters instead of sweatshirts. I actually even broke out the ancient, crusty tube of mascara in my bathroom and put on a little bit of makeup. I wasn't sure why; I was pretty certain that the majority of class would be spent in the dark, looking at slides.

"You look nice," Germaine said that morning over our cereal bowls.

"What's that supposed to mean?" I asked. I rarely drank coffee, but I was already on my second cup. I felt jittery.

"It secretly means you look awful," she said. "What do you think it means?"


As I crossed the quad later that day to get to the building where the class was held, I remembered what Mike had said about how I could be mysterious if I wanted to. While I didn't necessarily feel like trying to be an exotic nonstudent, I realized that nobody on campus knew who I was. Nobody here could look at me and tell I wasn't a student—that I had taken the year off, that I barely had any friends anymore, that I lived at home. For all they knew, I was the daughter of a famous person (Germaine had gone to school with one of Donald Trump's kids). Maybe it was a cool thing, and not a terrifying thing, that I was going into the situation with a totally clean slate, and no one around to say, "Oh yeah, that's Cecily: she fights with her sister, her hair looks like a Brillo pad when she wakes up in the morning, and she's had to see two professionals just to get here."

I was going to be whoever I wanted to be. I was determined to be optimistic about this.

I hiked up to the third floor of the building and found the classroom. It was hard to feel independent and confident when I was wheezing and my sweater was sticking to my back, but I purposefully chose a seat in the middle of a half-occupied row. The room was shaped like a small auditorium, and I looked straight ahead as I walked down the steps to my desk, instead of burying my chin in my chest.

I sat down, put my winter coat on the back of my chair, pulled a brand-new steno pad out of my messenger bag and a pen I'd stolen from Dad's office, and lined everything up on my desk. I looked around, trying not to crane my neck too much. There were about twenty other students in the classroom, all silent. Some text-messaged, some riffled through their backpacks, some stared off into space. There was nothing on the projector screen in front of us, no teacher at the podium. It would be difficult to be the brand-new Cecily Powell if I wasn't even in the right place.

"Excuse me," I said to a striking black girl with short hair sitting to my right, who was entertaining herself by staring at her furry boots. "Is this Intro to Art History?"

She looked at me and nodded. Not friendly or unfriendly. Just answering my question. I nodded back. The New Cecily asked questions and got answers.

"Hi, everyone, sorry I'm a little late," said the blond, mustachioed man who walked in and hurried down the stairs. "I'm Professor Gunderson. This is Intro to Art History. Let me just check on the slides and we'll get started."

The lights were shut off, I was bathed in a beautiful, colorful glow from what I think was a Picasso, and Professor Gunderson started talking. No attendance-taking or announcement-making, just talking about how he actually hated Picasso, but it was okay because he had reasons why, and here they were, and we shouldn't be afraid to dislike something, even if it's famous, as long as we could say why. I wasn't sure if I should take notes or what, but it felt nice to sit there in the dark and just listen.

**april**

**Work was boring,** but I enjoyed watching the first hints of spring appear through the windows of Dad's office every day. Buds started to bloom on the trees, and the wildlife (squirrels, that is) started making more of an appearance on campus. One fluke day it hit sixty degrees, and half of the student body was out in shorts.

And I enjoyed going to class. I wished that I could just take one at a time for the rest of my life, although I knew if I did, I would graduate about the same time I was supposed to retire. I never ended up getting to know any of the kids in the class; it was hard when so much of it involved sitting in the dark being talked at, but it didn't stop Dad. He was on a roll. He was convinced if he could simulate the college experience for me enough, it wouldn't be that hard to actually get me going.

"I'm thinking you should go visit your brother at Madison," he said one day on the way home from work.

"Why is that?" I asked. "I'm here, spending time on campus."

"Josh can show you around, show you what it's actually like to be a student," Dad said. "And I think living on a campus for a few days might help . . . unless you'd rather go visit some other schools." Dad had done this with Germaine back when she was looking at colleges: they packed up the car and looked at twelve schools in ten days. I don't know what went on during that trip, but I know that when they got back, they didn't speak to each other for two weeks, and Germaine ended up going to a school they never visited.

So it was decided. After checking schedules, I would go visit Josh in the first weekend of May, before he had to start studying for finals. "Don't worry, we're going to have a lot of fun, I promise," said Josh on the phone, as we solidified the plans.

"Cool," I said, trying to sound nonchalant. "I like fun." But truthfully I was nervous. I didn't mind spending a few hours on campus a few days a week, but that seemed like day camp compared to sleepaway camp. I was worried I was going to hate it and Josh and I would fight and I would come home and be less, not more, ready to move on.

"We're definitely going to have a party, so just make sure you look good," Josh said.

"I already look good," I said, looking at myself in the toaster. I was wearing a red hoodie, and I had the hood up around my face like Elliott from *E.T.*, although I could barely fit all my hair under it.

"Right," he said. And hung up.

A new challenge had been presented. Since I hadn't ventured out in public much since coming home over the summer, I'd paid very little attention to my looks other than my recent adventures in mascara. Back in high school, I wasn't, like, a fashion plate or anything. But I cared enough to know that I looked cute in little pretend-retro T-shirts, and while I hadn't inherited Mom's height, I had gotten her decent legs, so I tried to wear a skirt every now and then. I was putting a little more effort into what I wore lately just because I was on campus, but I hadn't purposefully tried to look cute since high school. There was no point in putting on makeup or picking out special outfits just to impress Germaine and Dad. Sometimes Germaine tried to shame me into taking care of myself a little bit more.

"I haven't seen that sweatshirt in a while," she'd say at breakfast. "I can barely remember the last time you wore it. Was it yesterday?"

"Leave her alone," Dad would say. She was probably just mad because she had to wear suits for work now. I was mostly relieved that somehow my sporadic attempts at exercise were keeping me from getting fat. I could still fit into my pants, so that was good.

But just because I didn't care what Dad and Germaine thought of my clothes didn't mean that I didn't care what a bunch of college kids would think. I was already going to feel out of place just by being there—I didn't want to look wrong on top of it.

There were three bathrooms on the second floor of the house. Dad had one attached to his bedroom and Josh and

I shared another, since neither of us really cared about that sort of thing. But Germaine's bathroom was her sanctuary. I didn't even really know what it looked like, since I swear she had set up bear traps and laser-beam triggers in there to keep us out. The last time I had set foot in it was when I was about ten: Meg had dared me to shave my legs, and I sneaked in to grab a razor. I must have replaced the razor about a millimeter off the mark, because Germaine smacked me in the back of the head when she found it out of place.

This, however, was an emergency. I was going to have to look hot. My own stupid brother had told me so. Josh's and my bathroom was disturbingly low on hot-making devices. I think motel bathrooms offered more amenities than ours, where the sole aim was simply not to stink. I owned a few bits of makeup—blush, some mascara—but I was always ashamed that they didn't seem to multiply in boxes and drawers the way they seemed to so naturally for other girls. I put my hands on my hips and glared at the ancient lipstick in our medicine cabinet, willing it to reproduce and provide me with liner and lip gloss on its own, but it just sat there, aging and drying out.

Kate had sent me photos of her and her friends "going out." That was the phrase she used: "going out," as if being outside didn't really count unless you were at a bar and wearing a pair of black pants. I thought that in college, you rolled out of bed in your pajamas and slunk around campus like that. Not these girls, anyway. They were all wearing the same pair of tight black pants, it seemed, the same skimpy little tank top in different bright shades, towering platform shoes, and lip gloss so shiny the flash bounced off their mouths. Their hair looked like it was parted with a knife and hung down around their faces. Two girls had curly hair that seemed like it was still wet, and three others, including Kate, had hair so stick-straight and dry that it looked like it could catch on fire at any moment. Their eyes were all wide, their smiles even and white and brilliant. I examined Kate to see if she was secretly rolling one eye or flaring her nostrils or something, but as far as I could tell she blended in with the others. Not that I blamed her for it. I wouldn't have minded having fun group photos to stick up around my room, to prove I did indeed have friends that I could be adorable with. Most of my cute photos were from high school graduation, and I had taken those down a couple months ago, although I had been fond of a picture of Mike and me picking each other's noses with our mortarboards.

Germaine had gone out with Conrad, so I cracked open the door to her bathroom. Sunlight poured in through the window as if it were some sort of holy shrine. Near the shower, a rainbow of bath gels and lotions and scrubs lined the shelf. I crept in, looking back behind me to make sure she wasn't actually at home, ready to spring on me. I examined the different varieties. Enchanted Apple. Sultry Musk. Sweet Pear. Ravishing Roseberry. I had no idea that fruit could be so slutty. And what the hell was a roseberry anyway?

I lifted the top off a lotion called Stem. It smelled sort of like cut flowers, very green and clean. I made a mental note to steal that when I left, but not until then or else Germaine would hunt me down and scalp me.

I stood at the sink and flicked on her cosmetics mirror, which lit up with about two thousand watts. You could practically see pimples that wouldn't even be arriving for another month. I opened Germaine's medicine cabinet and was impressed by the sheer organization of it all. A bouquet of Q-tips sprang from a tiny glass jar, so perfect and small I couldn't even imagine what its original purpose must have been. I couldn't figure out why one would need five identical hairbrushes, but they leaned out of a container I normally would have used to hold pencils. Lipsticks stood neatly on end in a long box. Eyeshadow boxes lay perfectly stacked on top of each other. I grabbed a few items that looked like they wouldn't be missed.

This seemed like the perfect time to pilfer Germaine's supplies, since she was distracted: she was officially moving out. She had found a place in the city with a girlfriend (she claimed it was her friend Melissa, but I had a feeling "Melissa" looked a lot like Conrad), and she'd be moving out by the end of the month.

I was a little surprised by how melancholy Dad seemed about Germaine leaving.

"I can't believe you won't be here every night anymore," said Dad at dinner one night.

"Oh stop, Dad," said Germaine. "I'll be fifteen minutes away by car."

"I know," he said, and chuckled thickly, a sound that meant he was choking back tears. I never thought that Germaine and Dad had a special bond the way he and I did. They didn't fight all the time, but they seemed to irritate each other on a regular basis. Plus, Germaine was the only one of us who was close to Mom, so I figured that by default Dad would not miss her that much when she left. So the moving out had seemed like a good idea, especially since I could get more time just hanging out with Dad and not feel like I was in Germaine's way.

He started sniffling again the next night at dinner.

"I'm going to be an empty nester," he said, gazing at Germaine. "I'm going to be a lonely old man."

"Yep," said Germaine. "It's going to be tough."

"I feel like I should carry you into your new apartment the way your mom and I carried you into this house."

"Oh for Christ's sake," I said. "I'm going to be here. And then I'm going to leave. Why don't you cry about *me* leaving?"

They stared at me. I tried to concentrate on cutting my steak.

Sometimes it made me sad to think about how little Germaine and I did get along. I know that most siblings, even those immature like me, would say, "Well, I hate my brother or sister, but I really love her." I was glad for Germaine, and also hoping that once we weren't around each other maybe we'd be able to cultivate one of those "Now that my sister and I hardly ever see each other, I love her!" relationships I'd always heard about.

What does that even mean?

This one time, though, we'd actually been sort of getting along, and I thought we'd have that heart-to-heart. I didn't know what I imagined, a TV show maybe, where we'd get everything out in the open and then hug and cry and maybe go shopping and get our hair done and eat candy, but that didn't work out.

Germaine had been home from college on a break and Dad was out of town on a conference, and she and Josh threw the obligatory party. It seemed like it was going to be crazy—even I was allowed to invite people. Germaine was actually introducing me to her friends, who got a kick out of asking me what high school was like, as if we were generations apart.

The party was going well. Josh and Germaine maintained good crowd control, so there were a lot of people hanging out in the backyard, eating pizza and drinking beer, but nothing was out of hand. Everyone was getting along, the music was good, and the neighbors hadn't called the cops or anything like that. I wandered out into the yard and saw my sister, sitting on an empty keg, smoking a cigarette out of an actual cigarette holder and talking to three or four guys.

"Hey, Audrey," I said.

Instead of keeping up her friendly front, Germaine rolled her eyes, but didn't look at me.

"I mean, like Audrey Hepburn, like from *Breakfast at Tiffany's*," I said.

"I'm aware of what you mean," she said, sniffing, ashing her cigarette and giving her boyfriends a look like, "You see what I'm talking about?"

"I *am* five years older than you," she pointed out, as if you had to be of college age to watch films.

"So, nobody's puked yet . . . I mean, as far as I can tell," I ventured, trying to keep up the good-naturedness. Germaine waved off her boys and turned to me with a look that meant she was going to give it to me. I tried beating her to the punch.

"Hey," I said, "what's your—"

"*What's my problem?*" she filled in. "Try this on," she continued. "You always make everything about you."

"I what?"

"*I what?*"

This was getting annoying. I was starting to wonder whether I really did sound like a baby when I talked. Plus, this wasn't the sort of tack Germaine normally took.

I said, flabbergasted, "What is with you? You know, why do you hate me so much?"

"Hmm," Germaine said, obviously savoring the speech that was coming. It was like she was sitting in front of a buffet and she couldn't decide where to start eating. "Let's see. You're spoiled. You don't take anything seriously, so when I try to actually talk to you, you act like a retard and run off like a banshee. You get special treatment because you're the baby." She took a giant drag from her cigarette and charged ahead. "You only want to talk about yourself," she continued, "so whenever I say anything about myself, you completely brush it off. You never ask me about my life. You tell the stupidest jokes and then you pout if everybody isn't utterly delighted. You interrupt people when they talk, and you don't let other people intervene when you talk; you just raise your voice louder and louder. And because you're so self-centered and such a little baby, any little accomplishment you do, anytime you wash the dishes without being asked to, everybody's supposed to react like you just split the atom, and when I fail to be enthralled, Dad acts like I just kicked his puppy."

"See, this, this kind of speech is not what I—" I tried to interrupt. But she was still on a roll.

"You utterly lack the adult concept of responsibility, doing something because you have to, not because you want to. As far as you're concerned, you can do whatever you want and let everybody else pick up the slack. And I'm the only person who happens to see this, and I hate it! I do everything I'm supposed to do, you do nothing, and you're still the goofy little baby. I can't stand being around you or talking to you or even thinking about you."

"Wow," I said, genuinely impressed.

"Oh, and you go through my shit," she said. "Don't think I don't notice, Cecily. You're not that fucking slick. Well, I've got news for you: you'd better watch your own back because maybe—"

"Okay, okay," I said. I didn't like the threats. "Well, do you want to know what I hate about you?"

"Fuck you, Cess," she said, jumped off the keg, and sauntered off.

"Listen to what Germaine just told me," I said grabbing Meg when I found her. We laughed about what a crazy bitch she was, which helped distract me from wondering about whether it was true. She hadn't yelled at me like that since, but it seemed like it was because she just didn't want to talk to me that much.


Germaine was moving out the weekend I was visiting Josh. I decided that it would be a good idea to see if she had some sisterly nugget of wisdom for me before we both left. We'd mostly been avoiding each other: she'd been busy with packing and work, and I was just trying to stay out of her way. Now that Dad was suddenly so sad about her leaving, I'd probably look like the bad guy if we had any fights.

The night before I was supposed to leave, I walked down the long hallway that separated our rooms and knocked on her door.

"What." Her voice came out in a monotone. I was already annoyed.

I opened the door with some struggle, because it always stuck. I couldn't tell if Germaine did it on purpose or she just radiated suckiness that spread even to the walls of her room. "Hey, I—"

"I didn't say *come in*," she said, glaring at me. She was sitting on her bed, reading a magazine, still in her work clothes.

"Fine!" I said, and shut the door. I was midslam when I realized that I was asking for help and I would never get anything from her if I pissed her off, so I caught the door and closed it softly.

"Hear ye! Hear ye! Germaine, I have come to ask thee sage advice on looking at colleges," I shouted through the door. "As you may know, I am going to visit our brother, Joshua, tomorrow in the state called Wisconsin and—"

"Jesus Christ, stop yelling. Open the door."

"Okay. Hi. So, I'm leaving soon, which I know you must be thrilled about, and Dad wants me to know what the hell I'm doing, and I don't. So, I don't know, I thought you might know something."

"Quit leaning against the door frame and come in and sit down. You're making me nervous."

"What are you reading?" I asked, sitting on her desk chair.

"I thought you wanted something, Cecily."

"Oh yeah, right. Well. You know. Dad's all gung ho about

this visit and all that crap and I need to get something out of it. I don't really know what to look for, though."

Germaine didn't react to this question at all, just leaned over to a drawer next to her bed, opened it, and took out a big dark green candle and a pack of Parliament cigarettes. "Open the window, will you?" I did, and she lit the candle and lit a cigarette, ashing into a pop can she had nearby. I wanted to ask her who she thought she was kidding: we all knew she smoked in her room, but I didn't say anything. I'm sure Dad knew she smoked but didn't seem to care as long as she kept it in her room and didn't stink up the whole house. I guess that that was part of her punishment for having to live at home, too, like a kid—sneaking around like a kid.

"Are you looking forward to it?"

"I guess. I mean it'll be nice to see Josh. And it'll be weird. But I guess it's something I have to do."

"Buy a T-shirt. Actually, get me a 'Fuck 'em Bucky' shirt if you see one."

"'Fuck 'em Bucky'?"

"Josh can explain it to you."

"Okay, a T-shirt. That's a good idea. I just don't want to make Dad mad and—"

"It's really not that big a deal, Cecily. You see the campus, maybe go to a few classes, check out the study-abroad office, see the gym, go to the bookstore. What else do you think you're interested in?"

"I don't know."

"Well, bullshit it. Pick up a school newspaper and see what they're talking about. Go see frat row or something."

"I don't think I can join a fraternity."

"Okay, I think this conversation is over, Cecily."

"All right. I guess I want to know . . ."

"What?" Germaine had picked up her magazine again, to signify that we were done. She huffily closed it, but with her finger between the pages.

"Did you like college?"

"Of course," she snapped. But then she took a thoughtful drag. "It's odd, sort of, being with all these strangers, but you sort of figure out who you are. It's your last chance to be irresponsible, too."

"What didn't you like?"

"I didn't like that I graduated and suddenly had no idea what the fuck to do with my life. They could have . . . I don't know, prepared us better. I don't know if you know this, Cecily, but if you stay here, it's eventually going to get less fun for you. Dad might give you pity points right now, but trust me, stick around and he'll get less patient. So it's in your best interest to go."

"Huh."

"What?"

"I guess I didn't think of it like that."

Germaine stared at me. "Are you high? What did you think you'd be doing? You know it's practically against Dad's religion to take time off from school, don't you? So whatever it is that you need to have figured out by the end of this year, do it quick, because I don't think you get more time to do it. If you want to go to Italy or Greece, call up Mom now."

"I don't know why you're so hot to hang out with Mom all the time. She hasn't been awesome to us."

"Well, *I* don't get why you like hanging out with Dad so much."

"Duh, I'm the favorite."

"Gee, you think?"

"I was just joking, Germaine."

She ashed dramatically into the pop can. "I'm just saying I don't think there's a coincidence that you always take his side and then he lets you stay home for the year. He would have never let me do that."

"Thanks."

"Cecily, eventually you're going to have to grow up and deal with the same shit that everybody else does. I'm just telling the truth."

"Okay," I said. "I appreciate it."

"You're welcome. See you later."

# may

**"Let's go!"** Dad cried. He clapped his hands with evil glee. "Wake up!"

The light was harsh and yellow and I hated him for a second. "I hate you," I muttered into the mattress. It was the day I was to visit Josh.

"What?" he said. "Did you say you want to take a shower? Okay!"

He practically ran down the hall, and I heard the shower turn on.

"The shower's on! Don't waste water! Go! Go!"

I sighed, squinted at him, and trudged to the bathroom and got in the shower, feeling heavy and sickly. As I got dressed, I smelled bacony goodness below, which drew me downstairs despite myself.

"A good breakfast to start your day," Dad said, placing a plate in front of me. It was still a little dark out, and gray

146

like the day before. The kitchen blared with bright light and NPR.

"The directions are pretty easy," Dad said, handing me a printout as I dug into a bacon-and-egg smiley-face man. He had even bought the hazelnut-flavored cream that I liked. I turned the coffee nearly white and added about three pounds of sugar to it. "I also put a copy in the car and one in your coat pocket, just in case. And I put a roll of quarters in the car so you will have money for the tolls in case for some reason the E-ZPass doesn't work."

"Thanks," I said, sopping up egg yolk with a bite of toast.

"There's also a first-aid kit in the glove compartment in case of emergency," he said. "And if you get pulled over, don't get out of the car. Keep the windows rolled up until the cop shows you some I.D."

"Dad, I've taken driver's ed. I even did well! I have this thing called a driver's license. It's like an award they give you when you finish."

He shrugged his shoulders. "Go brush your teeth!" He whisked the plate from under my chin. There was still one tiny drip of yolk left, but he put it on the floor, where Superhero cleaned it with one wipe. "Go!"

I ran upstairs to brush my teeth. I grabbed my duffel bag and went back downstairs. It was time to go.

"Cecily! Wait!" Dad came hoofing down the driveway before I even backed out onto the street. "Give this to your brother. It's for dinner and other stuff. I will be checking with him that he received the full amount." He handed me a wad of money. "And I love you. And I hope . . . ah . . . I hope you have fun."

"Okay, Dad," I said. "You know, I'm not going to China."

He rolled his eyes. "I'm glad to be rid of you for a few days. You stink."

It was time to go.

Within a few hours, I emerged in good old Wisconsin. I followed Dad's directions until I reached a small lake and a dome appeared on the horizon. I drove toward it and suddenly, after traveling the cold veins of the highway and passing roadside oases and crappy chain restaurants, I was spit out into a small town, with cute restaurants, cute theaters, cute stores, and young people strolling around. This was it. I turned right and found a parking space. I pulled out my cell phone.

After I'd described where I had put the car (somewhere near a bar, and a store, and a coffee shop), Josh found me and helped me with my stuff. I didn't recognize him until he came up to the car; he wore a maroon sweatshirt and his hair had gotten a little longer, curly and unrulier on top than usual, plus he had a few days' beard.

"Hey," I said, getting out of the car. I wasn't sure whether we should hug. We typically only hugged when we were expected to.

"Hey," he said. "Pop the trunk." Instead of hugging, he went to help with my stuff, which was more efficient anyway.

We walked down the street, turning and heading past a church, then some houses that looked like they should have been condemned, except that they all had neon beer signs in the windows, indicating to me that they were indeed occupied, either by college students or people who worked for the Miller factory.

Josh led me to a brick building, and we hiked up two flights of stairs. "Here we are." He opened the door. It had never really occurred to me that Josh could be living anywhere other than our house. Whenever I had heard about his freshman-year dorm, I just imagined a version of his room at home, only with a roommate. This was an actual apartment. The living room was carpeted in dingy brown, and the window looked out across the alley, so we had a good view of his neighbor's truck on cinder blocks. Josh flipped on a television, and soon the room was illuminated. It obviously provided the main source of light for the place.

"Jesus, Josh. How big is that thing?"

"You like it? It's a plasma screen. Oh, you should call Dad, probably," Josh said, handing me the phone. "He only told me, like, ninety times to have you call when you got in."

"Hi, love," said Dad after I called, and immediately, I heard Germaine screaming in the background about whether I had gone into her bathroom.

"Hi, I just wanted to let you know that I made it and I'm alive. Josh does not live in a hellhole and I drove the speed limit the entire time."

"Hold on a second," Dad said, his voice rising with annoyance. "I can't hear you because your sister is home and she's speaking right now." I heard the phone rattle and then "WOULD YOU SHUT UP?" I smirked at the phone.

"Okay, well, I'm glad to hear that everything is fine," he said, getting back on the phone. "Did you give Josh that cash?"

"I spent it at a strip club off the highway," I said, pulling the wad out of my pocket and handing it to Josh, who didn't seem to find it weird that I was handing him a bunch of money.

"Nice," said Dad. "Put your brother on the phone, please. Have fun this weekend, okay? I want you to look around at the campus and talk to people, but I want you to have fun, too."

Josh took the phone and asked Dad about a paper he was working on for class. I looked out the window. A couple of girls were lying on towels in the grubby yard across the street, listening to iPods, their tank tops folded up to show their blindingly white stomachs. It was only May, and it was cloudy.

"Well," Josh said when he got off the phone, "do you want a little tour of the campus?"

"Sure. Oh, before I forget, Germaine said she wanted a something Bucky shirt."

"Fuck 'em Bucky?"

"Yeah, I guess that's it."

He snorted. "What is she going to do with a Fuck 'em Bucky shirt?"

"I don't know, maybe she wants to give it to Conrad. Anyway, I've heard so much about these famous Fuck 'em Bucky shirts and I still have no idea what they are, so I'm just curious now what it is we're talking about."

"I'll show you," Josh said. "I'll buy Germaine's and I'll get one for you, too."

We walked down the street and turned onto the main drag, which was lined with bars, restaurants, and head shops, which had small clumps of dingy-looking kids gathered in front. We turned into one of the numerous college apparel stores named things like Badger Bin and Madison Madhouse. The store was brightly lit, and racks and racks of T-shirts and sweatshirts and shorts and mugs stretched to the back of the store. Clothing hung from round displays, on the walls, on shelves. It had the smell of fresh sweatshirts and iron-on decals. A local radio station blared a weird mix of heavy metal and hip-hop.

The university name was printed on everything, from underwear to child-size cheerleading uniforms to gigantic beer steins. My favorite was a T-shirt that said UNIVERSITY OF WISCONSIN on it over a pattern of Hawaiian-looking waves, as if surf was always up in the Midwest.

We reached the back of the store, and Josh pointed up on the wall. A handful of T-shirts featured a crabby-looking badger puffing out his chest, wearing a turtleneck sweater and turning up his middle finger (claw?) at the wearer. And they said FUCK 'EM BUCKY!

"Bucky?" I was dismayed to see a cute animal behaving so rudely.

We strolled around campus. I liked that there were some wooded areas and was intrigued by a hill that Josh said students used cafeteria trays to go sledding down when it snowed. He kept pointing out buildings that I instantly forgot the name and purpose of. The library, the arts building, the gym, the bad dorms, the good dorms, the frat houses. They were all nice, but frankly I didn't care that much about where people took their science classes or didn't.

"So what do you think?" Josh asked as we stopped in front of some hulking building so I could tie my shoe.

"It's very nice. Brick," I said. I hoped he wasn't going to give me a quiz like Dad, because I wasn't sure what this one was, even though he had just told me. The astrology building?

"No, I mean, you know. Overall."

"It's fine," I said. "It looks like campus back home, only different." This was true. It was even on a lake, although one inferior to Lake Michigan. "It's more spread out. But otherwise the same."

"Yeah," said Josh. "In a lot of ways, they're all sort of the same."

"That kind of sucks," I said.

He shrugged. I wished I were home.


Later, after we'd seen most of campus, Angie met us on the patio of the student union for dinner. It was still a little chilly and gray, but with our jackets on, it wasn't too bad out. It was nice sitting on the lake, even if it was a lesser lake than what I was used to. Groups of students, adults, and families with little kids clustered around the metal tables scattered about, enjoying the tolerable weather. I had to admit, I had been looking forward to seeing Angie. I had simply given up on trying not to like her.

"So, Cecily," said Angie, "do you think you might want to go here?"

"I probably won't—I didn't apply anywhere else, and it looks like Kenyon will take me back if, you know, everything works out. But I don't see why I wouldn't otherwise. What are the people like? Is it, like, a big party school?" I cringed saying that phrase.

"Sure," said Josh.

"It's not annoying?"

"Sometimes it is," Josh said. "But I just think that you can't really get away with a lot of the same stuff once you graduate, so I enjoy it. I mean, I hope I don't become one of those guys who is a college guy after college or anything."

"You probably will be," I said.

"Thanks," Josh said.


The next morning I woke up in Josh's bed and briefly panicked when I couldn't remember where I was. Then, when I did, I panicked again, realizing I still had another day to spend here, away from home. The room felt stuffy and hot. It was sure to be a long day.

After I showered (with the tiny dried-up sliver of the only thing in the bathroom that resembled soap), I stood in the steamy bathroom, almost crying from exhaustion as I tried to comb out my hair. I had forgotten a hairbrush, and the only thing available in the bathroom was a tiny black plastic comb, the kind they give out on class picture day. It was totally inefficient in my hair, which could be so thick sometimes that I was convinced a family of birds could live in it with no problem. I wondered if it would be acceptable just for me to leave the comb in there. Finally, I half combed it out with my fingers and pulled it back with a rubber band. By the time I was done, I was hot and sweaty.

Josh was sitting on the couch watching TV when I got out of the bathroom.

"You look uncomfortable," he said.

"I *am*," I said. "Thanks for asking."

"Well, I went and got us bagels while you were in the shower," he said. "One of the perks of getting up early on a Saturday: you get first pick, since everyone is still sleeping it off." He heaved himself off the ugly plaid couch to grab a coffee off the counter. Slightly mollified, I picked an everything bagel from the paper bag.

"Sorry to keep you from going out and getting hammered," I said.

"Well, I don't do it that much anyway," Josh said. "But I appreciate the sentiment."

"I didn't really know that was an option in college," I said.

"What?"

"Not drinking."

"Well," Josh said, stirring his coffee.

"But you drink."

"Sure. But not so much now that I'm dating Angie. We're not really the get-shitfaced-together kind of couple."

"What did you do before Angie?" I crammed bagel halves into the toaster and prayed that they wouldn't get stuck and catch on fire.

"Sure, I went out. I bought a fake I.D. It was the worst. It was from Wyoming, supposedly. The photo didn't even fit into the frame that well. There was a little space of just clear plastic to the side."

"Did you like it?"

"The I.D.?"

"No, going out."

"Sure. Why not? But after a while it feels like a routine, I guess. The same people going to the same places, dancing to the same songs. And I only really went out on the weekends; some people go out more than they stay in, so I don't know what that was like for them."

"What do you do when you don't go out and drink?"

"There are things to do on campus. Cheap movie night. Concerts. Some big bands and comedians come in." We settled on the couch and finished our bagels in silence as Josh channel-flipped on the huge TV. Part of me wanted to know if this is what I came for—hanging out on the couch, which I could just as easily do at home—but at least I was watching TV in a different state. That had to count for something.

After breakfast, Angie came by. She and Josh were going to multitask—showing me more of Madison while simultaneously buying supplies for the party that was to come tonight, the one that would inevitably publicly reveal my many issues and probably scar me for life. "Are you having fun so far?" asked Angie as we headed to the car.

"I haven't done much so far," I said. "But sure, I'm having a good time."

"Cecily isn't doing anything at home anyway," said Josh. "So this isn't much of a vacation for her. It's like a weekend-long playdate."

"What's that supposed to mean?" I asked. "And anyway, screw you. I've been working and going to class. I haven't just been sitting around." We had reached the car. Angie was standing in front of it, and Josh and I were standing by the driver's side. "What are you doing?" I asked.

"I figured I could drive," he said.

"I drove up here," I said. "I know how to fucking drive a

car." My face felt hot and I was embarrassed to be doing this in front of Angie.

"I know," he said. He stopped and tried again in a quieter voice. "I know. But I know the town better than you, and it might be easier if I'm driving than us yelling directions at you and stressing you out."

I looked over at Angie, who was carefully studying the hood of the car.

"Fine," I said, and handed him the keys.

I was ready to have a good, babyish mope in the backseat, but Angie wouldn't let me sit there.

"You kids are fun to hang out with," she said.

"Do you have roommates, Angie?" I asked as Josh backed out of the parking spot.

"Yeah," she said. "I live with five other girls. It's hell on earth."

"Jeez," I said. "I wouldn't be able to stand it."

"Yeah," she said. "It sucks unbelievably. And the thing is, they're all—well, they're mostly—all my good friends," she said, "and we still are. But we just can't live together."

"How come?" I said.

"Oh you know," said Josh. "They're always stealing one another's boyfriends and being prettier and thinner than one another."

"I wish that was all bullshit," she said. "But that's some of it."

"What's the rest of it?"

"I think it's a little easier when you are just in a dorm room, because there's less to worry about. It's one room," she said. "But when you're in an apartment, there are more common areas. There are groceries to worry about, and the kitchen. And some people don't know how to do dishes, which is fucking pathetic when you're twenty years old. Like, wouldn't you think it was bad to put dishes away when they still had food stuck to them?"

"That doesn't sound good," I said.

"Also," she said, "if you saw that the garbage hadn't been taken out for weeks, and there were bugs walking around the garbage, would you take it out? Or would you ignore it until somebody else did it?" Her voice was getting louder.

"I will have to think that one over," I said.

"I think girls think that living together is going to be this nonstop slumber party. You know, hanging out and doing each other's nails and eating chocolate and watching sappy movies and holding each other's hair back when we throw up. But it's not like that at all. The pressure gets to you, so instead of dealing with it a normal way—the way a guy would, to say, 'Dude, take out the trash'—girls get really passive-aggressive. I do it, too. I don't take the garbage out, either. You know why? Because I'm making a statement that I won't do it. Nobody is noticing it, of course, so it just makes me mad instead. And then, when somebody borrows my curling iron without asking, I blow up at them because I'm so pissed at them already."

"Then," said Josh, "there are the groceries."

"Oh yeah. My roommate Christie is the only one with a car, so we have to go with her every time we go to the store," said Angie. "Look, by the way, there it is." We circled around the Capitol, which looked like every other capitol building in the country: it had a dome.

"Whoo," I said.

"Anyway," Angie continued, "it's a big hassle and everybody goes their separate ways once we get to the store and we always end up buying too much stuff to fit in the car. And then people eat one another's groceries and get into fights."

"They each have to buy their own milk," said Josh.

"Seriously?"

"Yes," she said. "Because God forbid that somebody drink Lola's special soy milk. Or somebody touch Evelyn's two percent milk. And then for those of us who drink whole milk, somebody always leaves like a milligram at the bottom and doesn't replace it."

"So you drink whole milk?" I said. "Gross."

"No, I am totally off milk because of all that," said Angie. "I pour water on my cereal and I drink beer with my cookies."


After shopping and lunch, Angie went to the library to get some work done, and Josh and I collapsed on the couch and found a marathon of shows on TV that educated us on how great the seventies were. He promptly fell asleep. I watched a few episodes, learned a lot more about *Wonder Woman* than I had ever before. I dozed off sometime during 1976 and woke up to my brother pressing a cold can against the back of my neck.

"Beer!" he yelled. I wished I could just go back to sleep and let the party happen around me. I could be very good at pretending to sleep. I felt too warm, too cozy, too nice and safe for a party.

"You know, Josh, I'm not planning on getting all crazy," I

said, sitting up. "I'm not going to dance on the table or break something or make out with a bunch of guys or throw up or take my clothes off or something. So you can stop making the googly party-girl eyes at me because even though I'm the fun sister, I'm sorry, I'm just not that much fun."

"Are you *mad* that I'm throwing you a party?" His voice didn't sound that angry, but the clang the beer can made when he put it down on the fake wood coffee table did.

"It's for me? Seriously? I never asked for a party, Josh." I thought of the coming-out parties that I imagined occurred all the time in the South. I don't know why it was only the South, but that was how it was always in my head. Sixteen-year-old girls emerging from Tara in elbow-length gloves and beehive hairdos and saying, "So nice to meet you, Mistah Smith," and then getting engaged. That was the abbreviated version. The long version involved dancing Virginia reels and drinking punch and much more dialogue.

Josh snorted and turned the TV to a basketball game. I had that horrible sibling moment where you force yourself to say something nice even though you don't want to.

"I'm sorry," I said. "I am excited. I guess I'm also nervous to meet all your friends. And I'm nervous that if I don't do something right I'm going to have a terrible time and embarrass you."

"Cess," he said. "I'm going to be honest with you. Dad told me it was really important to show you a good time this weekend. *Really* important. It's a party. It's not a test or anything. I might stress out just because it's my party, but don't let that affect you. Don't worry about it so much, okay? You've been overthinking everything lately, or something."

"You're right," I said. "You're nicer about this than Germaine is."

"Why, she's been giving you shit?"

"Eh, kind of. I dunno. I can't tell if she's mad that I'm taking a year off. Or just that I'm around."

"She's just hating because she would have wanted a year off."

"Well, she should have taken one."

"I don't think Dad would have let her," said Josh. "Me, either, for that matter."

"Really?"

"I think he was tougher on Germaine," Josh said. "I mean, what do I know, but I get that impression. She might be, I dunno, bitter."

"Huh," I said.

"Yeah. Drink your beer," he said. We heard some shouting outside. "Freshmen are always the first ones out," said Josh. "I remember when I got here, the first weeks of freshman year, sort of drifting around at night desperately trying to get into whatever parties upperclassmen were throwing. I mean, it was only two years ago, but it feels like it was forever ago. It's kind of embarrassing. Nine hundred of us would go outside and meet up with nine hundred other freshmen and drift around like a swarm of gnats. We'd hear there was a party at one house, go over there and all act like we knew whoever was throwing the party, real suave-like, and run over to the keg and practically suck out whatever foam was left in there.

"We all looked like jerks, I'm sure, because the freshmen this year look like jerks. But I remember not really enjoying the experience: not enjoying the people I was with, or trying to sneak into parties, and certainly not begging for crappy beer. But I think I thought that if I didn't go out, then nobody would know who I was and I would have no friends, and that I would have lost my one shot. Is that totally lame? It is, isn't it?" he said, taking a drink from his can. "I guess my advice to you is, when you go to school, don't go out just because you feel like you won't be cool if you don't. Because you probably won't have a good time, and you'll just feel stupid, I think." I hoped I wouldn't feel that way tonight.

I went to the refrigerator for a refill and headed to the bathroom with beer in hand to shower again before the party. What was my problem? This was going to be fun. I was witty and weird and fun and so was my brother, and everyone was going to be delighted to meet me. I allowed myself to sing a little in the shower.

Afterward, I went into Josh's room to put on some fresh jeans while he headed into the shower. I came back into the main room and wondered if it would be greedy to get a third beer. Even if I wasn't actually having a good time, I was doing a good job of convincing myself that it was a possibility, and I didn't want it to go away.

Somebody then came out of the bathroom who sort of bore a resemblance to my brother, only a lot gayer. He wore dark jeans that looked expensive and a navy striped button-down shirt that was open a little bit at the top but with no undershirt. And he had shaved and put something in his hair. He was wearing cologne. Not a lot, but I could definitely smell it.

I fell off the couch laughing.

"What's so funny?" asked Josh.

"You're very pretty, that's all," I said, trying to catch my breath. "And you smell like a manly forest in autumn. Very nice."

"Don't hate," he said.

There was a knock at the door.

Angie had on tight, dark jeans; sexy heels; and a low-cut, deep purple top. She was wearing eye shadow and lipstick and looked like a completely different person. She looked good. But I think I probably would have taken a few hours to trust her if she was dressed like this when I first met her. It was a little intimidating. I realized I looked like crap.

"Have you guys been pregaming?" asked Angie.

"Cecily refuses to call it that," Josh said. "But yes. Do you want a beer?"

"Sure. What have you been up to?" she asked, sitting down. She sparkled and shined and smelled good. I wanted to throw up.

"Nothing. I'm wearing the wrong outfit," I told her. I was pretty much wearing what I'd been wearing all day long: a variation of what I usually wore to work, a black sweater and jeans. It hadn't occurred to me to seriously change outfits. Probably because Josh's apartment didn't look like it was about to have a party in it, other than the booze and the few bowls of snacks he was starting to put out. Also, I didn't know that you dressed up for a party at somebody's house. I should have asked Kate where she had bought her black pants and tank top.

"Aw, you're fine," said Angie.

"No," I said. "Help me."

"Okay, okay," she said. "What have you got?"

"Not much," I said. "Help me. I don't need to look sexy. I need to not look stupid."

"You don't look stupid," she said.

"Come on," I said. "Please."

"All right, all right," Angie said, taking me by the hand and leading me back to Josh's room. She grabbed an extra beer from the fridge.

"The boots are fine," she said, taking one of them out of my duffel bag. "Actually, they're kind of hot. And the jeans will do."

She dug around in the bag. "Boy, you're organized. How about this?" She pulled out a basic black tank top.

"I usually just wear that under sweaters or whatever. It's not very special or anything."

"It's fine," she said. "Seriously, you don't need to worry about this so much."

"I just don't want to look like . . . I don't know. I want to blend in, I guess. You have to know that as we speak, you're seeing the side of me that makes me very weird, the reason why I'm not in college. So I apologize. I hope you don't hate me now. I don't always act like this." My face burned.

She laughed. "You're fine. Believe me, I'd rather be helping you out with this stuff than hearing my roommate complain about her yeast infection."

"For real? Ech."

"For real," she said.

"Just don't make me look like a freak," I said as we headed to the bathroom. I don't know why I was trusting Angie with all this. What did I know about her anyway? She was dating my brother. What did that make her an expert in? Well, she did have a boyfriend, was going to parties, and was in college, so things were obviously working out better for her than they were for me.

"Oh, first you want me to help you, now you think I'm going to make you look like a freak?"

"No," I said. "Look at my hair. Just look at my hair. It's pathetic."

"Drink this," she said, handing me the beer. "Pull out your ponytail holder."

"My hair's wet," I said. "And I don't have a hair dryer or a straightener gel or pomade or whatever the hell I'm supposed to have."

"I didn't know you had such cute curly hair!" she said, fluffing it around my face.

I made a face in the mirror. "It's stupid," I said. "That's why I usually pull it back." My hair made me look like eighties Cher.

"You never wear it down?" she asked.

"No," I said. "I never got used to it. I had straight hair until I was about eleven or twelve and then *boing!* It just got like that. I don't know why. I never figured out what was up with it, and I don't care to. Sometimes I straighten it, but only when I have four or five hours to kill."

"I would die for this," she said.

"You can have it."

"Hold on." She opened up the cabinet and got out a little jar.

"What's that?"

"It's your brother's. It's what he uses to keep his own lovely locks looking so curly and cute." Angie took a few fingerfuls of goop and ran it through my hair. It smelled like grapefruit.

"All right. So just don't comb your hair. Or touch it. It's going to look adorable."

"Okay," I said. "What about my face?"

"Well, we can't do anything about that, I'm afraid," said Angie. "We'll just cover it up with a bag and hope everything goes all right."

"You're hilarious. Okay, so I stole some makeup from Germaine. I have no idea what I took, though."

"Let's see what we've got here," she said, poking in the makeup bag, which was decorated very stupidly with little high-heeled shoes and sunglasses and lipsticks. Like a makeup bag was so inherently butch that somebody really needed to dress it up to look feminine.

"This will be good," she said. "Close your eyes."

I did and felt her patting something on my eyelids, gently but purposefully.

"You're good at that," I said. "I think."

"Mmm," she said, concentrating. "Okay, I'm going to put some eyeliner on, so I'm going to stretch your eyelid. Don't freak."

"Just don't stab me in the eye." She placed a fingertip on the corner of my eye and pulled it to the side slightly, and I felt the pencil on my eyelid.

"I gotta say, if Germaine was my sister, I'd be stealing makeup from her also," said Angie. "She's got good stuff. Okay, mascara. Open and look up."

I opened up my eyes, and she came at me with the wand. I caught sight of us in the mirror and started cracking up.

"What's so funny? I almost swiped this all across your face."

"I don't know." We could pass for friends going out for the night, normal girls who did normal girly things together, like getting ready for a night out. It was fun but somehow embarrassing.

"Cecily, I can't tell if you like it or you don't."

"I do like it. I haven't . . . I don't know." I couldn't take my eyes off myself, actually. The eye shadow was a silvery charcoal that was smoky without being too dark and made my eyes look intriguing. I hadn't seen my bare arms since the summertime, and it looked like my sporadic trips to the gym had helped. And I was pleased with my hair: it was still voluminous but looked under control. And it felt so good to spend fifteen minutes with someone and not fight or talk about college or myself. But I felt strangely bashful and was wary of assuming that Angie was my new best friend all of a sudden. Maybe I should call it a night while the going was good, before I messed anything up.

"You look cute. Not too done up. But cute."

"Yeah," I said. "I have to admit it."

"Give it up," she said. "Give it up for Cecily. Give it up for me."

"I'm giving it up," I said.

We heard some voices in the next room and some thumping around. "Sounds like the guys are here with the keg," Angie said. "Are you ready to break some hearts?"

"Shut up," I said. "You're going to make me self-conscious. I'm trying to act natural."

We opened the door, but there was no *ta da!* sound; life

did not change to slow-motion so that the guys in the living room messing around with the beat-up keg could stand up and ogle me as I confidently, unself-consciously glided out of the room. I almost tripped when I came out, actually, which was fine because the guys still didn't look up until Josh introduced me.

"Guys, my sister Cecily," said Josh. "Cecily, that's Paulie, George, and Dave." One was bald; one had longish, greasy hair; and one was cute. In that order. The guys were impressive, sort of scary. They reminded me of the senior football players from when I was a freshman in high school. Like having a herd of buffalo pass by you a few times a day, they were intimidating and interesting, yet I knew I'd never get to know them. But here they were, talking to me.

"Hiya," said George.

"Aww, you and your brother look alike," Dave said after shaking my hand. He looked like he could have been Mike's hunky older football-playing brother. I bet if I asked him to carry me around the rest of the night, he could and wouldn't get tired. I wondered if he would.

"Hi, boss," said Paulie to Angie. "How's Christie? Is she coming by later?"

"Not if I can help it."

"Paulie is in love with Angie's roommate," Dave explained to me.

"Seriously, dude, the next time you sleep on our couch, keep your pants on," Angie said.

"I get hot," he said.

Josh opened the door, and I heard a piercing scream. I nearly had to cover my ears. I had forgotten that sound, the sound of girls who scream. If I had to say one good thing about my sister, it was that she wasn't a screamer. I hadn't heard that noise since high school graduation, when we all did it.

"Hey, bitches!" said the screamer, a short, skinny girl whose movement into the room I could only describe as "bopping." She bopped into the room. She was wearing an extremely short black skirt and a bright yellow tube top. Her hair was long and straight. It was somehow not blond but not brown, either. It was blah.

"Dave, you are such a dick," she said, pointing at him. "And you know why." Before he had time to respond, she asked Josh, "Is Sharky coming tonight?"

"I believe so," said Josh. I looked at Angie. I think it was the first time I'd ever seen her look anything other than pleasant.

"Yes!" squealed the girl. "Sharky! Have you ever met Sharky?" she asked, suddenly turning to me.

"No," I said. "I have not."

"Well, you'll love him. He's such a fucking riot!" I didn't know who this girl was, so I had no idea how she might think I might like this person, but I couldn't lie and say I wasn't intrigued.

"What's so great about Sharky?" I asked.

"Who is this bitch?" asked the girl, pointing at me but smiling.

"Beth, this is my baby sis, Cecily," Josh said.

"Aww, the baby! How old are you?"

"I'm twelve years old," I said, feeling only twelve when introduced that way.

"Shut up!" said Beth. "Are you really?" she asked.

"No," I said. "But I was, once." She doubled over, laughing. Either I was drunk or I was the funniest girl in the Midwest. Maybe both.

"I'm going to piss myself!" she screamed.

"Well, who exactly is Sharky, then?" I asked, feeling exhausted.

"Sharky's a lot of fun," said Angie, smiling at me. "He's a, um, character."

"I was going to live with Sharky until I found out that he had a problem peeing in people's closets," said Josh. "That's sort of the first thing you'll learn about him."

"Gross," I said.

"Sharky's really generous, though. He found that chair in his alley and brought it here for us," said Josh, pointing to a ratty-looking armchair that I had been avoiding all weekend.

"When he's really drunk, he break-dances," said George.

"If you're lucky, he'll dance with you!" said Beth.

"Great," I said. This night was getting extremely silly, and it was still early.

I heard a heavy knock, and Paulie opened the door. On the other side, approximately nine thousand people were all waiting to get inside, get drunk, talk to my brother, dance to music, make out, get sweaty, and possibly touch my things.

"Ow!" cried Josh. "What are you doing?"

Without knowing, I had gripped his arm as the door opened. I guess I gripped it kind of hard.

"Can I go?" I whispered. "I can find a coffee shop or a bookstore or something and hang out until the party is over."

Josh laughed, as people poured in the general vicinity of

the keg and the unceremonial stacks of red plastic cups. "No way," he said. "Sharky's here!"

I looked over to the doorway, expecting to see Paul Bunyan or the Jolly Green Giant or at least somebody who looked mythical and larger than life, but instead I saw a short, stout guy, built like a fire hydrant. He carried a bottle of what even I recognized to be cheap whiskey. His body was a perfect rectangle. His face resembled a bulldog's, flat and sort of mean-looking. I didn't care how fun he was supposed to be; he looked scary to me.

"Cecily, this is Sharky. Sharky, this is my sister—" Josh said. But before I could say anything, I was looking down at the party. Sharky, despite his shortness, had picked me up and lifted me over his head. I felt the breath pushed out of my stomach and for a second I had reconciled myself to the fact that I was going to barf on this guy's head.

"Put . . . me . . . down," I tried to say, but I could only whisper.

Finally, he pretty much dropped me on the floor, and I had to act like it didn't hurt too much, although it did.

"He's sort of a human tornado," said Dave, flashing a perfect white grin and all-American good-lookingness in his navy polo shirt and thick brown hair. "Impressive to observe but painful to get in the way of." He extended a hand toward me to help me up. I was sort of getting a little crush on him.

To their credit, neither Josh nor Angie left me alone during the party, which had been my greatest fear. One or both of them was next to me at all times, introducing me to people. And I had to admit it, most of the people were nice. They actually seemed excited to meet me, excited to tell me about funny things Josh had done, excited to see if I was going to go to Madison. They looked like normal people. Were they actually this nice, or were they just drunk? I couldn't tell.

Speaking of drunk, I wasn't. Too much, anyway. I felt a nice, warm buzz, which seemed to indicate that more beer would be even more fun, but Josh wouldn't let me drink that much more. Which was a shame when Dave, who continued to be cute, tried to get me to do a shot of tequila with him. "You smell nice, you know that?" he said. Borrowing Germaine's lotion was totally worth it.

"I think she can wait and do it on her own time," said Josh, drinking the shot himself. "She wouldn't appreciate it."


The party was hardly the all-night experience I thought it was going to be. After a few hours, the keg was finished. About half the people had left the party, but the half who stayed started hitting the hard alcohol. Some had paired up doing gross grindy dances. Paulie was playing some sort of card game with some other guys. I turned into the kitchen to see if I could steal a beer from the fridge. There was Dave, making out with Beth. I stood there for a second and realized that I was staring at two people kissing, so I stuck my head in the refrigerator, pretending that I was looking hard for something. Failing to find what I was not looking for, I split. Neither one of them had even noticed that I was in the vicinity.

This, I realized, was one of those times where it would be good to have a female friend around. Someone who was my friend, who actually knew me, not one I had borrowed from my brother. Had I thought that Dave was going to kiss me? Be my boyfriend? Fall in love with me? No. But I still felt upset. I had let myself have a teeny, tiny one-night crush on a boy, probably the first time I'd done that since Mike. (Who was I kidding? I had been in love with him all along. This party was almost over, and it was time to get real.) And it ended up as nothing. I figured that another girl would understand that sort of thing.

I had been a little tipsy earlier, but I suddenly lost the feeling and now was sick of this place. Where was all the fun? I went to go find Josh. I stepped over Sharky, who was lying on the floor on his back, still clutching his enormous bottle. I thought he was unconscious, but as I walked over him, he grabbed my leg.

"Hey," he said.

"Yes?"

"You look so good it hurts," he said, and to demonstrate, he put his hand over his heart.

"Thanks," I said, and pulled my leg free.

I walked back toward Josh's room, and the stink of the apartment, smoke and beer and sweat, started to get to me. Everything I saw was irritating me. The ugly carpeting, the scratchy used furniture, the striped shirts the guys were wearing. There was nowhere to go but this place and nothing else to do but just be here.

Germaine had told me: I had no choice, I was going to have to join these people. I'd have to leave home, spend Dad's money, start dating some idiot, have friends who always found things to shriek about, and move on through adulthood. It sounded like such bullshit.

"You look like you're having a lot of fun," said a voice. I turned around and saw Angie.

"It's okay," I said. "Kind of weird."

"Pooped out?"

"Yeah."

"Want to get some food?"

"That sounds like the greatest idea ever," I said. "What about Josh?"

"He can tend to his party, as long as we bring him something," said Angie. "I'll go tell him we're going out. Go get a coat."


"You okay?" asked Angie as we walked down the street back to Josh's apartment, eating big floppy pieces of pizza on paper plates. We'd gone to a pizzeria that served slices with different kinds of pasta on them. Mine was topped with macaroni and cheese, and I hoped the moment would never end.

"Yes, I'm better. So, like, I guess. What do you do here? You know. You seem like a normal person. What's your life like?"

"What do you mean?"

"I mean, I don't know. Do you belong to a sorority?"

Angie snorted. "Hell no. Like I need one more thing in the world to piss me off: a bunch of girls I don't even want to be friends with turning me down from living in their nasty house. If you want to meet someone who is in a sorority, you can talk to Beth. Beth is in SDT," she said. "That's a sorority, and everyone jokes that it stands for 'Spending Daddy's Trillions,' but I don't know what it really stands for. Sorry."

"That's okay. What about clubs? Are you in any clubs?"

"Clubs?" Angie thought for a second. "Oh yeah. I guess there are clubs here, aren't there? No, not those, either."

"Oh," I said.

"College isn't really like high school," said Angie. "Mostly you just do whatever you're really interested in, you know? Sometimes I go on community service trips or something like that, help do food collections and stuff. But I'm not doing it so that when I graduate, I can say on my résumé that I did that. I don't think people really care about that when they're giving you a job. I think that college is training wheels for real life. You're more independent than you are in high school, but you sort of still have people looking after you, unlike when you get to the real world and you're on your own."

"Hmm," I said. I couldn't tell if that sounded good or bad.

"For the first time, you can do whatever you want as long as it feels like you're doing it because it's you. It takes a while to find out what that really means, of course. Sometimes you think you're doing something because you think it's fun, but you realize you're just supposed to. So it's cool when you realize what you really want to do and what things just aren't your scene. But it's not, like, mind-blowing or anything. I won't lie, when I left for school, my dad was like, 'Have fun, because these are the best days of your life.' And I am having a lot of fun, but that's pretty depressing if these are the best days of my life. I think my older sister is having the best days of her life. She lives in New York in a shitty little apartment and has a job that's killing her, but it seems awesome." She smiled and was quiet for a second. "I'm really relieved that we get along," she said.

"Oh whatever," I said, getting shy all of a sudden.

"I think Josh was excited to show you a good time. And I think he was nervous, too. I think your dad might have put some pressure on him to, you know, show you around and all that."

"I guess that makes sense." I felt embarrassed, realizing what an idiot I must have looked like to Angie. And yet she still liked me, or seemed to. "I'm just nervous. I don't know about what, even. And that's what worries me, that I should have had stuff figured out by now. I feel like a big baby."

"Cecily, *everyone* feels that way when they start school. I mean, yes, it's exciting, and you should look forward to it. But it's also scary as hell. Anybody who acts like they're not scared or that they have any idea what they're doing at first is totally lying. Things will be awkward for you probably at times, but they are for *everyone*—that's the best thing I can tell you, that you might feel out of place at first but so does everybody else. And things just get more fun after that."

"They'd better," I said. But I had to admit it: I was having fun on a college campus with a few people who actually seemed to have personalities, and it didn't hurt too much.

We then heard some screaming, and three naked guys came racing down the street and into the night.

"Ah, college," said Angie, and something in her voice sounded affectionate and yet embarrassed at the same time. I started laughing, and laughed hard.

# june

### "Rx: Sister."

"Hmm," I said to Jane. "Can I refuse treatment?"

"Come on," Jane said, glowing from a perfect summer base tan. "You know you can do this stuff now."

"She probably doesn't want me there anyway," I said.

"I think you blow the animosity in your relationship out of proportion," she said. "And anyway, I think you need to reach out to her. You pretty much just don't talk to her or your mom, right? Do you think that's healthy?" I shrugged.

"You and your mom will have to work things out one day," she said. "But I don't think it'll be that hard to try to just hang out with Germaine. You might need her one day. Or she'll need you."

"She'd need me for a kidney," I said.

"Or you might need hers! See?"

Dad loved Jane's idea and thought it would be nice for me to go visit Germaine in her new place, which I still hadn't seen. Going to check out some strange, sad little apartment was not going to be fun for me, and I'm sure Germaine wasn't looking forward to spending time with me. But Dad wouldn't be stopped. He even volunteered to set it up.

"Because, it'll be *nice*," I heard him explaining on the phone to Germaine. I'm sure she was wondering if it was a trap.

I think he just wanted me to get out of the house. Dad and I had finally had our fight, a fight resembling what I thought had been coming since the second I turned around from the dorm room door. And since neither of us seemed to have the balls to talk about it directly, it came out of something stupid.

"Cecily, Superhero needs to go for a walk," Dad had said a few days earlier, coming into my room as I was doing some art history reading.

"I just took him out," I said, which was true. Sometimes Superhero was a filthy liar.

Dad sighed heavily. I put the book down.

"What?"

"What do you mean, what?" Dad said. "Your dog wants to go out."

"I JUST TOOK HIM OUT."

"You know, I don't ask that much of you, Cecily," Dad said. "Especially this year. I think I've given you a lot of room. I just don't know what's up with you."

I'd had it. There was nothing *up* with me. "You know what? I was always good. I'm maybe not as perfect as Josh, but I think I've been doing pretty fucking okay. I'm not a bitch like Germaine. And I didn't sleep around or get fucked up or even get bad grades. And just because I didn't do this one thing—no, it's not that I didn't do it, it's because I didn't plan on it—everybody thinks I'm nuts? Well, fine, maybe I am, but whatever, I don't think I am. I think you just need to lay the fuck off me and let me do my own thing. I don't know what that thing is yet, but Jesus Christ, I'll get to it, okay? Now where is the fucking leash?"

I clapped my hands to get Superhero's attention, stormed out the door, and headed out toward the lake path. I fumed: it felt good to be mad. Typically, whenever I thought Dad was mad at me, I felt sick to my stomach. If he ever seemed disappointed in me, I wanted to kill myself. But I didn't feel that way.

After the fight, we ignored each other for the rest of the evening and ate dinner quietly in front of the TV. Since then, we had been avoiding each other and gradually pretending that the fight didn't happen, so it was nice to have this visit for Dad to arrange to get me away from him on a weekend.

In Chicago, summer comes later than it does for the rest of the country. When Dad took me to hang out with Germaine, we'd finally had our first week of warm weather. The sun shone so brightly that the glare off the lake was making traffic on Lake Shore Drive slow down. We exited near a giant Indian totem pole that, for some reason, stood in the park between the high-rises and the water. Dad turned onto a little residential street lined with trees and old brick apartment complexes. Couples strolled down the sidewalk. I would rather live in a neighborhood like this than on a college campus.

"Be good, have fun," Dad said as he dropped me off.

"I'll try," I said, opening the car door. "I will," I amended my statement. Why not? If Germaine really didn't want me over, she wouldn't have allowed me to come over. And Angie had said that her sister was having the time of her life living in the city and working at her job. Maybe Germaine was, too. Maybe we would have fun.

I hit the doorbell with our last name next to someone else's and was let in with a loud, obnoxious buzzing. As I opened the door, I wondered if Germaine had picked the building on purpose for the annoying buzz. It sounded uncannily like her voice.

She lived in a big brick apartment complex, with a dark, dank hallway inside. I hiked up to the third floor, wondering how long the stained old carpet had been on the floor, and whether the windows on the stairwells opened, or if they had been painted shut forever.

I got upstairs, and Germaine was laughing.

Not at me, though. She stood in the doorway with her phone to her ear, laughing at something being said on the other end of the line. She looked good. She usually wore her hair down, flat-ironed and straight, which I thought looked really severe. Now it was pulled up in a messy half-ponytail-half-bun, with parts of it flying around her face. She wore a pair of red running shorts and a lime green T-shirt and stood in her bare feet. I hadn't seen her since she moved out in

May; she looked like she'd lost some weight. She looked like she had been exercising, which was very unlike Germaine.

She waved me in, barely glancing at me, and said, "What? No. Really?" She gestured with her arm to mean, I think, *Have a look around.* I had some flowers with me, which were also Dad's idea, but I had no idea what to do with them and Germaine was clearly engrossed in her phone conversation, so I walked around, holding the flowers like some pathetic lover boy.

Once I started looking around, I had to admit, the place was kind of cool. The building was old, there was too much white paint chipping off the windows, and there was permanent dust in between the cracks on the hardwood floor. But the windows were flung wide open and sunlight poured into the living room. Little knickknacks covered the shelves and the small mantel over the decorative fireplace. Tiny little vases and plants and figurines. Were these Germaine's? I was in her room at home so rarely that I couldn't remember what she had in there, or what she liked. I checked out the bookshelf, crammed with old paperbacks, many with an orange sticker on the spine that said *USED.* A lot of poetry and philosophy.

"Hey," Germaine said, coming back into the room, now off the phone. "Sorry about that."

"Who was that?" I asked.

"No one," she said, and I wanted her to ask who the flowers were for, so I could say, "No one," but she didn't.

"These are for you," I said instead.

"Oh thanks," she said. "These are pretty. Let me go put them in some water."

"This is a nice place, Germaine," I said, following her into the kitchen.

"Yeah," she said. "We like it."

"Who? You and Conrad?"

"What? No, remember, I'm living here with Melissa?"

"Who's Melissa?"

"Just a friend from high school."

"I don't remember her."

"I wasn't really friends with her in high school. She and I rode the same train to work and got to talking and we started hanging out and decided we'd move in together."

"Oh," I said. The kitchen was packed with containers filled with rice, spices, chocolate chips, and some grains I couldn't identify. The pantry was stuffed with boxes marked "All-Natural" and "Organic."

"Is this all your stuff, too?"

"No, most of it is Melissa's," said Germaine. "She's really into cooking. We've already had a dinner party and a cookout so far. You should come sometime."

"Really?" Then a small orange cat wandered into the kitchen. "What's that?" I asked.

"That's Mr. Henry," Germaine said. "He's Melissa's."

"No, not who. What is that?" I said. "Since when are you a cat person?" We had never owned a cat in our family, ever. And neither had my mom and neither had my dad. Cats were a weird tradition that some other families had that we never practiced.

She shrugged. "We thought it would be fun." She pulled a blue glass vase out from under the sink, filled it with water, and stuck the flowers in. "So, do you want the tour?" she said.

"Sure," I said. "Sure, I'll take the tour. Nice to meet you, Mr. Henry." The cat looked at me and then looked away.

The apartment had a porch in the back, which seemed rickety compared to our nice little patio back home. There were too many layers of brown paint and there was a lot of dirt, it seemed, but Germaine and Melissa had made the spot look nicer with some flower boxes and a little wrought-iron table and chair set. The whole back of the building looked like a cute little community. All the other porches were adorned with dangling ferns, barbecues, herbs in pots, wind chimes. "Sometimes we sit out here on Sunday mornings and drink coffee and just talk about the weekend," said Germaine. "It's so nice."

Germaine's room was small—there was barely enough room in it for her bed, but a window next to her bed was open so that the breeze blew about a sheer white curtain, which made everything look more intimate than cramped. Also, her bed was new—we had twin beds at home but Dad had bought her a queen-size, and she'd debated for a long time before deciding to splurge on some designer sheets. I bet I could spend a whole day lying there, watching that curtain from under her fluffy powder blue duvet cover on the huge bed.

Melissa's room featured a big four-poster bed, with red gauze strung between the columns. It looked like something I probably would have begged for when I was eleven. I was secretly jealous.

"I have to tell you, I really thought you were moving in with Conrad," I said. "I thought you were just making up Melissa for Dad's sake so he wouldn't go ballistic."

"Conrad and I broke up," Germaine said, smiling.

"I didn't know that," I said. "I'm really sorry."

"No, you're not," she said.

"Well, sort of. I've grown accustomed to his face."

"Yeah, right. It was right after I moved out," she said. "I think he was mad that I wasn't moving in with him."

"Why didn't you?" I asked.

"Because he's a loser," she said. "I hate to say it. I mean, he was really nice. And really cute. But he didn't do anything."

"Yeah," I said.

"And I feel like such a yuppie, but when I finally started working and thinking seriously about moving out, I think he got jealous or something, like I was betraying him by getting a life." Like Kate did to me.

"You've gotten to be kind of responsible, haven't you?" I asked.

"Sure," she said, irritable again. "Why wouldn't I be?" But her crankiness was amusing this time, like she was Oscar the Grouch. I didn't take it personally, and she didn't really seem to be that mad.

Suddenly, I had a real reason to be sad about going to college. It seemed like there was a glimmer of hope that Germaine and I might actually start getting along like human beings. And I was going to be leaving.

"What time is Dad coming to get you?" Germaine asked. I'd been there about a half hour.

"Not for another hour," I said. "Do you want me to leave or something?"

"No!" Germaine snapped, and then softened, tried again. "I mean, no, don't be silly. I was just asking. Do you want some iced tea?"

"Sure," I said. We headed back to the kitchen, and she poured two glasses. We went to sit outside on her deck. It was actually adorable as hell. Someone in a big hat was kneeling over a flower bed in the courtyard below. Two guys with huge arm muscles were drinking margaritas and grilling on a balcony across the way. Germaine waved to them.

"This is really good," I said. I usually hated iced tea: it was the blandest of drinks. But this was minty fresh.

"Thanks," Germaine said. "So, uh. Your year is almost up, huh?"

"Yeah," I said. "Yeah, I guess it is. Time flies." Or did it?

"Do you think you . . . you know, figured everything out?"

"Absolutely not," I said. "I don't have anything more figured out than before. But, well, I'm not nervous. Right now. I'm nervous that I'm not nervous. I don't know."

"I feel kind of bad for you," Germaine said, pulling a cigarette out of a pack that was sitting on the table. She offered me one, and I waved it away. "I bet a lot of people think a year off sounds like a lot of fun, but you had to feel all this pressure to figure out life. And you can't do it in a year. You can't do it in a year at home, anyway."

"You're right," I said.

"I still would have traveled," she said. "Although I don't think traveling abroad for a year when you're eighteen is the same as doing it when you're twenty. I don't know." Germaine had spent a semester in London when she was in college, which I kind of thought was cheating, since I thought the whole point was to go somewhere where they didn't speak English. But, obviously, what did I know?

"I guess," I said. "It's hard to know what I don't know. You know?" I was trying to be funny, sort of.

"I know," Germaine said, but she didn't seem like she was playing along. "You're pretty spoiled." I took a big gulp from my iced tea, because I didn't know what that meant.

"But I'm also pretty spoiled, I guess," she said. "Dad let me sit around at home for a while without doing anything, too. Maybe I don't give him enough credit sometimes. That was sort of nice of him. I had friends who had to work through college and everything, or went to their new jobs the day after they graduated. The time after college is just tough. You're in school and you're in this make-believe land where you can do whatever you want, and then you come out again and it's the real world. It's a hard adjustment."

"So do you miss college?" I said.

"Not really, actually," she said. "I love my apartment. I even love having a job—I mean, it'd be nice if I had a more exciting one, but I like that when the day is done, I can just go home and do whatever the hell I want and not have homework or projects or anything like that. And I like that I can stay in on a Friday night and not feel like I'm missing out."

"That's what I'm worried about," I said. "I'm worried that I'm going to have to pretend to have fun when I don't want to."

"You're not pretending to have fun," said Germaine. "It *is* fun. But when you get out, you realize that there are many more kinds of fun out there. You didn't seem like you had that much fun this year."

"I had some fun," I said. "I liked visiting Josh. It was nice hanging out with Dad."

"But come on, Cecily," she said. "You had a whole year with practically no obligations. You had the year off! Do something with it."

"I was figuring stuff out. I worked," I said, suddenly wanting to put her cigarette out on her hand. "I took a class. I sort of traveled."

"Come on, Cecily. I think that whatever it is that you think is so safe and nice is actually holding you back. Have a little fucking fun before it's too late," she said.

*"Too late?"* This conversation was freaking me out.

"Not too late," she corrected herself. "Don't worry about that. It'll never be too late. Just . . . I think you'd regret it if you didn't make an effort to enjoy yourself a little bit more."

"I'll make a mental note," I said, polishing off my tea. "Have more fun."

She laughed, but I wasn't kidding.

# july

**"Do you think I'm spoiled?"** I asked Jane, seeing her for what was supposed to be the last time before I left for Kenyon. Unless everything fell apart again.

"Um," she said.

"Thanks a lot," I snapped.

"Hang on," she said. "I was just saying 'Um,' for God's sake. I do that a lot."

"My sister says I'm spoiled."

"Why do you care all of a sudden what your sister thinks?"

"I don't know," I said. "I guess I'm worried that that's why I screwed up, and that's why I didn't end up talking to too many people this year."

"I don't think it's that," she said. "I do think you're privileged, like a lot of the kids in this town are privileged. I think your problem, maybe, is that you haven't put yourself out there enough. You haven't had big challenges so far, in my opinion. You didn't think you were up to college because you'd never had to go outside your comfort zone before."

"Whose fault is that?" I asked. "I demand to know who."

She shrugged. "Let's not lay blame on anyone," she said. "Although, yeah, I do think your Dad might have, you know, let some things slide for you. He liked the relationship he had with you and didn't want to mess it up by pushing you too hard."

"But that's why we get along so well," I said.

"Well, life's crazy," she said. "He let you take the year off. He could have made you go. But on the other hand, you did all these other things that you didn't think you could do, or wanted to. You got back in touch with your friends even though it was easier not to. You went to class. You visited your brother. It sounds like you were able to see your sister without punching her."

"Yeah," I said. "I guess . . . even if we don't get along all the time, it's good to talk to her because I can see what's in store for me. After-college awkwardness and then a cute apartment?"

"Is that a question?" Jane asked with a grin.

"Maybe? Aren't you expecting me to have a revelation about how Germaine and I really love each other and maybe we're actually the same person or something?"

"What? No. That's weird. I just think family is important and you should have given her another shot, since I think you assumed she was the enemy if she was close with your mom."

"You're an evil doctor," I said, and Jane tried to laugh villainously, which was hard to take seriously when she was wearing a cute little black-and-white polka-dotted dress.

"Well, fine," I said. "I didn't like everything I tried, though."

"I think you went into a lot of it expecting not to like it, don't you think? You didn't exactly go full throttle—you could have done a better job getting out there and socializing, for instance. But you're not going to like everything you try," she said. "That's the point of trying stuff. Some turns out great; some, not so much. Do you think any of these things have really hurt you, though?"

"I guess not," I said. This was turning out to be one of those times when it wasn't too fun to talk to Jane.

"Not everything in college is going to be fun, Cecily. You're going to get your heart broken. You'll do badly in a class. You might get fat or have a bad roommate. But I guarantee down the line you'll still feel good about most of the things that happened, even if you don't feel good about them at the time."

"Germaine said something else," I said.

"What was that?"

"She said I should 'have a little more fucking fun' before the year is up."

"I don't think that's such a bad idea."

"Um."

"Now *you're* the one saying 'um.'"

"Seriously . . . I don't know what to do."

"What do you mean?"

"I mean, yeah! I want to have a little fucking fun. But I don't know what to do. What do I do?"

"You've *forgotten* how to have fun?"

"Well . . . yeah . . . kinda. I never had to generate fun on my own. You know, I'd do something with Kate or Mike or whatever."

Jane shook her head. "That's the saddest thing I've ever heard. We're right next to one of the best cities in the world. Go to a baseball game. The Sears Tower. The Art Institute."

"That sounds a lot like *Ferris Bueller's Day Off*."

"You could do worse. They had fun in that movie, didn't they?"

"Yeah. And a car got wrecked."

"Then take the El."

"Boy, you just have an answer for everything, don't you, Jane?"

"I guess I do," she said, and handed me a note.

"Anyway, I'm just rusty, is all. I needed some time to sort some shit out, right?"

"I think you've done enough sorting for now."

I read Jane's note: "Fun! Try! Good luck!" was the prescription.

"Our time is up." She stood up, still a few inches shorter than me in her red, strappy high heels, and stuck out her hand. I gave a handshake I thought Angie would approve of.

"I think you'll be okay, Cecily. You just have to believe you'll be okay. Or better yet, don't think about it at all."

I shook her hand. "We'll see. I'll give you a call in a few months if it turns out I'm living in a halfway house."

"Goody."

I walked to the reception room for what I hoped was the last time. Gina was working a piece of gum very noisily.

"I'll see you later, Gina," I said as I headed toward the door. "I just want to thank you for all the support you've given me this year. I'll never forget you."

"'Bye, Sally," she said without raising her head.

Mike had come home for the summer, but I hadn't seen him much, since he had a job downtown. True to his word, he had kept in touch pretty well since I'd seen him in January. I didn't feel as weird about it, either, once I had started working and taking the art history class. I actually had things to talk about. He had enjoyed his second semester at Kansas. He liked going to basketball games. He was digging psychology courses. And he had started seeing a new girl named Kim, but "very casually," he stressed. "We've just hung out a few times. She seems nice. I'm not really trying to rush into anything serious, though. That hasn't worked out so well for me."

"Casual? Does that mean you dress down whenever you see her? It's not black tie optional?" I had to make jokes to keep myself from feeling too jealous. Then again, maybe Kim, or whoever he saw, felt jealous if he ever talked about me.

I called him up the day after I saw Jane.

"Hey," I said. "Let's have some fun."

"Okay!" he said. "That's a hard invitation to turn down."

"Awesome!"

"So . . . what are we going to do?"

"I don't know," I said. "That's all I've got so far. I'm supposed to have some fun before I go back to school."

"I think that's a good idea, and I'll be happy to help you have fun. What do you want to do?"

"We could go to Great America."

"Don't you hate roller-coasters? And fanny packs? And churros?"

"That's true," I said. "I don't even know why I suggested it. How about, um . . ." I was totally going to cheat. "Maybe a baseball game, or the Art Institute, or the Sears Tower?"

"That sounds like *Ferris Bueller's Day Off*," Mike said.

"Oh does it? I've never seen that movie," I said. "But seriously, doesn't that kind of sound like a good idea?"

"You know what?" Mike said. "It does sound pretty fun. When are we going to have said fun?"

"How about tomorrow?"

"Sounds like a plan," he said.

"I'll e-mail you," I said.

I went online and ordered tickets to the White Sox game, and asked Dad if I could borrow the car. He seemed confused at first about what I was up to.

"I'm having *fun*," I said. "Get it?"

"I think so," he said. "I think I've heard of fun. I think you used to have some and then it went away."

"Hmm," I grunted.

I picked up Mike the next afternoon. He was wearing baggy khaki shorts, flip-flops, and a University of Kansas T-shirt.

"So now I guess you're all into UK, huh?" I asked. "For now, anyway."

"It's laundry day," he said. "And hell, yeah. Rock, chalk, Jayhawk."

"I have no idea what you're talking about. Project fun commencing!" I yelled, and rolled down the sunroof. A drop of rain hit me on the head.

"That can't be a good sign," said Mike.

"Project fun continuing!" I said, rolling up the sunroof, and we headed toward Lake Shore Drive.

The Sears Tower was not that fun, actually. After paying a ridiculous price for parking, we were herded into a room-size elevator with a bunch of tourists and whisked up to the 103rd floor. But instead of being inspired by the magnificent views, all I could see was cloud, and some smokestacks in Indiana.

"This is kind of boring," I said.

"I don't feel too good," said Mike, backing away from the railing.

"I just don't think there's that much to see," I said. "I think this is why they only spent a few minutes here in the movie."

"Do you mind if I go downstairs?" said Mike.

"Are you afraid of heights?" I asked.

"Apparently I am," he said.

"Yeah, let's go," I said. "Wow, I didn't know that about you—and heights."

"Now you know," he said.

"I feel so close to you, Mike," I said, squeezing him around the middle.

"I'm going to puke," he said.

"Leaving! Leaving now."

The Art Institute went a bit better, although we realized that it was the first time that either of us had gone without a class or our parents. I had just found out the week before that I had passed my art history class (as opposed to failing, so I felt like quite the winner) and was ready to show off my skills.

"Where do we start?" Mike asked, our voices echoing inside the big marble hall. "I used to like the medieval weapons when I was little, but I don't think I need to see that."

"Ooh, wait!" I said. "I know something." I pulled him upstairs past a big bronze, muscular nude statue ("That's what I look like naked," I said as we passed it) to the huge *A Sunday on La Grande Jatte*, the painting of a bunch of French people strolling around on a sunny day in a park in the middle of the Seine. Then I told him everything I'd learned about it in art history. Not very eloquently, though.

"Um, so this is by Georges Seurat, and it's influenced by the Impressionists, but it's actually Post-Impressionist. And if you look closely, you can see it's actually made up of little dots. That's called pointillism. A lot of people think it's just a picture of a really nice day, but other people think it's a representation of social tensions between city dwellers of different social classes, who, like, gather in the same public space but don't, you know, communicate."

"Very impressive," said Mike. "Did you read that off the card on the wall?"

"What? No! I learned it in class."

"Well," Mike said, leaning forward, "it pretty much says all that stuff right here next to the painting."

"What the hell!" I said, and then lowered my voice. "I don't get what the point is of learning this stuff in class if you can't impress people with it and make them feel bad for not knowing it. I think they should remove the thingies from the walls."

"You know what else?" Mike said. "This is the painting they were looking at in *Ferris Bueller's Day Off*."

"Is it?" I said. "I guess you're right. No wonder it looks so familiar."

After the Art Institute, we headed back down Lake Shore Drive, south toward Sox Park. "I'm excited for a hot dog. And fireworks," I said.

"And baseball," Mike said.

"Yeah, that, too," I said. "I hope it doesn't rain."

Of course, the skies opened the second that we took our seats, which were just barely beneath the small, flat roof. Rain poured down two inches past my knees. I stared at the fat guys on the field running to unroll the blue tarps.

"It might let up," said Mike.

"I'm getting a hot dog," I said.

After we devoured two delicious, smoked grilled-onion-covered kosher hot dogs apiece, it rained harder.

"I'm not sure I feel like sticking this out," I said. "Are you mad at me?"

"No," Mike said. "Not at all."

I had brought a tiny travel umbrella with me, so we were only half soaked when we got back to the car.

"I'm afraid this day has been hit and miss, funwise," I said. "But thanks for coming with me."

"Hey, I thought it was pretty fun," said Mike. "We saw a lot of things." His cell phone rang.

"Hey, girl," he said as he answered it. "What's up?" I tried not to eavesdrop as I pulled down the visor to look in the mirror. I took the rubber band out of my hair so that it could dry in a normal fashion without getting too frizzy.

"You should wear your hair down more, you know that?" asked Mike, once he had said good-bye.

"Aw," I said, and hoped I wasn't blushing.

"It looks nice. Anyway. I think I know where we can have a little more fun tonight."

"Where?"

"A party."

"Oh yeah? Where?"

"Meg's house."

"Ugh. No," I said.

"Come on."

"Mike, no. Seriously. It's okay. I'll drop you off, and you can go."

"It's across the street from your goddamned house."

"So?"

"What else do you have going on?"

"A lot, thank you very much," I said.

"Cecily," he said. "It's going to be fun. I wouldn't take you there if it wasn't going to be fun. When was the last time you saw anyone from school?"

"School."

"You need to come."

"You need to shut up."

"Don't be such a fucking baby," Mike said. "Maybe I'm not the best person to dispense advice on how to live your life, but this seems like the kind of thing that would be good for you to do. And I don't want to be friends with a shut-in anyway."

I was quiet. I wasn't sure what the problem was myself. I had proven that I could hang out with college kids. I had a friend to take me to the party. It wasn't like I was afraid of there being any kind of fight with the people there. But I just wanted to go home and watch TV. And not see Meg.

Kate and I met in high school, but Meg had been my friend since grade school. Until about the end of junior year in high school, when suddenly she became this totally fake bitch. Also she made out with Mike one night and didn't tell me about it for four months.

I used to hang out with Meg and Mike separately until junior year, when the three of us were in a study group together in history. I didn't really notice, maybe, how much fun we were having, working and taking breaks to look at the yearbook and make fun of people. But Meg did. We began hanging out more together, the three of us, going to movies and a few concerts at the Metro, this noisy dark club in Chicago that was relatively close and located in a busy-enough neighborhood that Dad thought was safe if we had a male chaperone. One night Meg called up Mike and they ended up hanging out at his house. They listened to music. They kissed.

"I just thought you should know," she had eventually told me. Our friendship was already strained at that point. We seemed to be pissing each other off more—I thought she was acting irritable and bitchy; she claimed I was immature and rude. She had asked to have lunch together that day, which I thought was kind of weird since we hadn't eaten together for a few weeks. We were sitting on a park bench downtown eating chicken wings, trying not to get too messy.

"I don't know if I still like him," Meg said. "But nothing else has been going on. I just—"

"Thought I should know, thanks," I said, cutting her off. "Anyway, I gotta get back to class." I tossed my bag of bones in the trash and walked back to school, leaving Meg with her car. I never brought it up with Mike, he never brought it up with me, and it was all much easier, since he didn't seem to be hanging out with Meg anymore after that anyway.

Meg and I never had, like, a huge door-slamming, face-slapping, all-out fight. But after she told me that she made out with Mike, I think I talked to her about two more times, ever. It had been a little awkward avoiding someone who lived so close to me, but it's easier when she's trying to avoid you, too. I don't think Meg wanted to have to explain or apologize, which was fine because I didn't want to hear it.

"What do you think everybody thinks of me?" I asked suddenly, as we got closer to my house.

"Honestly? Nothing. I'm sure they'll be happy to hear what you've been up to."

"What's everyone going to be talking about?"

"Themselves. Each other. You. All about you, Cecily, everyone's going to be talking and laughing and pointing at you."

"Shut up," I said.

"Seriously, based on the other parties I've been to this year, you mostly have your people who are just happy to see each other and catch up. There are a few people who are going to try to act like they're all cool now, like maybe they think that they're more impressive because they drink or lost weight or lost their virginity. And then a lot of other people just seem cooler than before. Less high school bullshit."

"Should I change my clothes at least?" I was wearing a denim skirt and a black tank top. I had wanted to be comfortable on our fun day but not look too much like I was a complete tourist. So the black socks and sandals and short-shorts and the visor and the camera on a strap and the CHICAGO: MY KIND OF TOWN! T-shirt were out.

"No," Mike said. "You're fine. If you're going to be like this, I'm going to ditch you."

"Don't you dare," I said.

We drove up to my house and pulled into the driveway. I ran to the back door and yelled up to Dad's office, "Hi, Dad! I'm home! I'm going with Mike to a party at Meg's house!" Superhero tried to poke his head out the door, and I had to push him back inside.

"What?" Dad yelled, but I closed the door and ran back to meet Mike by the garage.

"Let's go."

"Well, you're suddenly all business," Mike said.

"I'm so nervous I could poop," I said.

"Why?"

"I just feel weird," I said. "But I'll deal with it. You're right. I shouldn't be such a baby."

"You'll be fine," Mike said. "People will either be happy to see you or not recognize you."

"That's reassuring," I said. "Besides . . ." But before I could even finish my thought (not that I really had one), we were already across the street at Meg's house, a modern white stucco rectangle broken up by a smaller rectangle of huge wooden doors. The rain had finally let up, leaving a fresh smell in the air, but the humidity remained. My back felt sweaty. I wasn't sure what to feel more nervous about: the party itself or seeing Meg. Fortunately I didn't have much time to think about it, as Mike was pounding on the door before I even had a chance to peel the shirt away from my back.

"Hey, Cecily," said Meg, looking me in the eye as she opened the door. She waved at Mike as we walked into the front hall.

"Hey," I said back. We didn't hug or anything, but the second we said hi to each other, I realized I didn't have a problem with Meg anymore. I had no idea what she had been up to. I didn't even know what school she went to.

"What have you been up to? What school are you at?" I asked. "You look good." And she did. She looked a little slimmer than I remembered in high school, and she had cut her hair into a long sleek bob and straightened it, too. She looked like her own cool older sister. She had a long, upturned nose, and she used to wear her hair in big blond corkscrew curls, very sproingable (although she hated it when people—other than some guys—touched her hair), but now she looked prettier, more sophisticated.

"You know, same old school stuff I'm sure you're dealing with," said Meg, which either was a mean joke or meant she really didn't know what I was up to. "I'm at Barnard. What have you been up to?"

"Not much," I said. I wasn't technically lying, but I figured if we were going to bond, it would happen at a later moment. Realizing that I hadn't really spoken to her since junior year of high school made me realize that I couldn't really be mad at her, because I didn't really know her anymore. I think I felt ready to talk about my year, but I didn't want to mention it casually. It felt good when Mike listened and gave me advice, not so much when Kate offered uselessly that everything would be fine.

"Well, come in, enjoy yourself. There's a keg in the kitchen if you want," said Meg. I looked behind her and saw a swarm of kids, some I knew, some I didn't, gathered around something, so many of them you couldn't even see what it was. It reminded me of those pictures of piglets fighting for room when they're feeding from their mother.

Mike and I began to push through the crowd in the kitchen, because even though we weren't hitting the keg, you still need some sort of beverage to hold onto at a party. I felt like I was having some sort of flashback as we moved past a bunch of people, a mix of people whose names I knew, whose faces I recognized but didn't know, and whom I couldn't tell if I knew or not. Then somebody shrieked my name.

"It's so good to see you!" Kate said, lurching through a few people and hugging me. She was wearing some white eye shadow, and it looked pretty flashy. Still the good hugger at least.

"I know!" I said. "I'm glad I came." And I was, until a few more kids trickled in behind us and Kate widened her eyes in joy and opened her mouth huge, showing all her teeth.

"It's you!" she said, screaming and throwing up her arms in the direction of someone behind me. I didn't even bother to look to see who it was. I let myself be shuffled more into the house to make room for the people behind me.

Meg's house looked the same. Her mom had married Rudy, a fellow who was big at the Board of Trade. They'd been married since Meg was about eight. Rudy wasn't a bad guy—he just had sort of extravagant taste. The front hallway was all mirrors, and the floor was tiled with huge slabs of marble. It was nice and twinkly at night, though. Meg and I used to like tap-dancing on that floor when we were little.

It was weird—I had already forgotten a lot of kids' names—other kids from our class who I had known just from going to school with them for four years, from hearing their names at announcements or reading them in the yearbook or having a gym class with them. They'd seemed like they were an essential part of every day, but now that I hadn't seen them for a while, I'd completely forgotten about them. I was pretty sure these random people were thinking the same thing about me. There was that pretty, moon-faced girl who acted like an ethereal hippie and who everyone knew was a big slut. There was the ugly moon-faced girl that I had two years of English with who had an annoying laugh. There was that cute brown-haired, brown-eyed girl who always wanted to know if she was doing better in school than I was. I was surprised that she was at this party. Did that mean that she was as cool as me now? I always thought I was at least cooler than her.

I caught Kate's eye again from across the room. She waved me over.

"Hey! I'm heading out to another party. You're welcome to come with."

"No," I said. "This is enough for me, thanks. Whose party?"

"I don't even know," she said, looking at the girl she was with, whom I didn't recognize. The girl shrugged and didn't look at me.

"Yeah, that's okay. Thanks for the invite, though." I felt like it wasn't really an invitation, of course.

"We have to catch up sometime!" she said. "I can't wait to hear how the rest of your year was. It's been so long!"

"Yeah," I said. "It has, huh?" I wasn't sure when the last time was that we had actually talked. I looked her in the eyes, searching for the old Kate, old funny Kate who could take or leave any kind of party, who didn't need other people to tell her she was awesome.

"What are you looking at?" she asked, glancing away. I'd never seen her look self-conscious before.

"Nothing," I said. "See you around." She gave me a one-armed hug and was out the door with a slam.

"She's changed, huh?" said a voice behind me. I turned around, and it was Meg.

"Yeah . . . she has," I said. I wasn't sure what this was. I was worried this was like one of those times from junior high when Meg would try to get me to say something bad about one of our friends and then she'd go tell them. Though would it matter if Kate found out I thought she had changed?

"You guys still talk a lot?" she asked.

"Um, not so much," I said. "Part of it is me, though."

She nodded. "Yeah, me, too. We hung out a few times during the year, but I couldn't keep up with her, really. I mean, I like to have fun and everything, but I just get exhausted running around and partying all the time."

"Clearly, you hate parties," I said, raising my voice as some guy in the living room was attempting to play the piano with his butt.

She laughed. "Well, this is a special occasion. It's good to see everyone back here."

"Let me ask you something," I said. "What percentage of the people in this house would you say are your friends?"

"I don't know," Meg said. "Twenty-five? Maybe? I'm counting casual friends. But if I'm counting people who are likely to stick around and help me clean up afterward, like three or four."

"I'm probably not going to stay and clean up," I said. "But don't take that to mean I'm not glad to see you."

"I'm glad to see you, too, Cecily," Meg said. "I'd like to catch up sometime, for real."

"That's doable," I said. "I'd like that."

"What's your e-mail address?" she said.

"Actually, I think it's about to change," I said. "What's yours?"

"You can find it on the Barnard site," she said, and then we heard a splashing noise from the backyard.

"Shit," she said. "I told everyone *no swimming*!"

"Go tend to your party."

"Talk to you sooner rather than later?" she asked. I nodded.

Mike was talking to some girl I recognized from the class ahead of us. I couldn't remember her name, though.

He glanced over at me for a second and then turned back to the girl, but then he did a double take. "Okay," he said. "Give me a second. I'll walk you home."

"You don't have to walk me home," I said. "I was just saying good-bye."

"Wait for me by the door," he said.

I walked around Meg's empty living room. I hadn't seen

much of the rest of the house at the party, but this room hadn't changed since the last time I was there several years earlier. Meg's mom and Rudy had decided that this room would be decorated in an Asian theme. It was cool, with lots of little blue-painted porcelain knickknacks all over the place. It felt very Zen, whatever that really meant. There was a little clay stool against the wall that kind of looked like a bongo drum. I sat on it for several minutes alone, listening to the party go on in the rest of the house.

"You okay?" asked Mike when he found me.

"Yeah," I said. "I'm okay. I think I'm going to head home."

"You want me to walk you home?"

"Nah, I'm cool. Thanks."

"That wasn't too bad, was it?"

"I guess it wasn't." I wasn't floating home on a cloud of intoxication and happiness, but I didn't feel bored, or out of place. I felt . . . fine.

"So," I said. "One question. Maybe I should have asked you this earlier. But what's college *like*?"

*"Like?"* Mike shrugged. "Um, I dunno. It's not *like* anything. I guess it's the biggest cliché that ever happened, because everything you expect is there. But at the same time, it's pretty cool, because it's happening to you. I guess? Maybe I'm just cynical."

"I love you for being cynical," I said.

"Seriously, more than anything else, I'm looking forward to next year," he said. "It just gets easier once you do it for a while, once you fake it and figure stuff out. You just have to get through that stage and that's really not so bad anyway. Don't worry, Cecily. I'm not worried about you."

We hugged good-bye.

I walked home, still feeling surprised by how calm I felt. I'd entered that party without nearly as much trepidation as the party in Wisconsin, and Josh or Angie weren't at this one. And I wasn't drunk—I had pretty much faked it as a normal person at this party. One who, even if I didn't belong, at least didn't *not* belong. I had faked it and come out fine. And I was okay with that.

# august

**I figured before I left** I should check in one last time with someone from my panel of experts, just in case. I sat down to the computer:

*Leah—I'm starting again soon at Kenyon. Yes, I'm trying there again. Like I said, I don't think it was the school that was wrong, it was me that was wrong. I guess I'm ready this time? Do you have any words of advice for me before I leave? —Cecily Powell*

A few hours later, I got a return e-mail:

*Nope. ☺ Drop me a line when you're home for Thanksgiving. —L.*

Well, that was anticlimactic. But at least she seemed to believe I'd have a Thanksgiving break—I wasn't completely sure yet. Last year I assumed that I would experience the same rites of school as everyone: registering, exams, Thanksgiving break. But every time I contemplated it, a voice in the back of my head this time said, "Are you *really* going to do all that stuff?"

"YES," I'd say out loud, and Superhero would look up and wag his tail.

There wasn't much left to do except start packing up again. There was the stuff I had taken to Kenyon last year, things that I'd never even gotten out of their original packaging. I carried some of the boxes up from the basement and opened them. It felt a little like Christmas. I had seen it all a year ago, but I had already forgotten that I had some of these things. I had bought a children's alarm clock that woke you up with the noise of a shrieking monkey. My roommate was sure to love that. (I had gotten a letter from the school. Her name was Lauren, and she was from Georgia. I didn't try to contact her, and she didn't try to contact me. I figured nothing good had come from e-mailing with Molly. And maybe Lauren and I would have more to talk about when we met.) A red lamp that clipped onto your desk or bed and had a bendable neck. A yellow corduroy "study pillow" that Dad insisted I buy, although I had no idea what it was really for. My new comforter, which had a nice wavy striped pattern of chocolate brown, lime green, and light blue. I had been deciding between that and a really weird blanket that was white with a huge lobster printed on it—I had figured that at least I'd own a conversation piece—but in the end I decided to go a little more mainstream. Dad had suggested that I take Germaine's old flowered pastel Laura Ashley comforter, but if it was possible for a girl to feel emasculated, that comforter would have done it for me. The sheets I had to match were still in their packaging. I bet they smelled nice and plasticky. Nervousness was now mixed with the excitement of remembering my new stuff.

In addition to all the new supplies, I had to decide which parts of my actual life I'd be taking with me. Last year I had packed a ziplock bag of inside jokes and trinkets and photos from high school: ticket stubs and postcards and collages that I had collected, to put up on my wall in my dorm. I had unpacked the bag but didn't put anything back up on my bedroom walls. The pile now lay in a drawer in my desk. It didn't feel right to take those to college, to pretend that they were still my life.

There were now three photos on the wall next to my bed. The first was a cute one of Josh, Angie, and me from the party in Madison I decided to take with me. I might never look that good again—unless I hired Angie as a personal stylist—and it was nice to have visual evidence that at least once over the last year, I had a good time with friends. The second picture was one of Superhero wearing a pair of sunglasses. Obviously I packed that one. The third was a picture of Kate and me on graduation day. We were doubled over in laughter about something, her long auburn hair falling around her shoulders in two perfect segments. I looked at it. I left it. I suppose that most people who saw it wouldn't know that it was taken over a year ago, as opposed to a few months ago. But *I* would know. It felt kind of pathetic to bring it along just to make it look like I had more friends than I did. Besides, I had the picture of a dog wearing sunglasses. Clearly, even without the lobster blanket, I would be the most popular girl on the floor.

I'd quit working at the end of July so I could spend the rest of my time packing and filling out the rest of the paperwork I needed to start school again. Like last year, though, I tried to squeeze in as much downtime as I could. Probably after a whole year of not doing much, plunging into five classes a week was going to be a nightmare.

Mom had sent me a letter that I wasn't supposed to look at until I was on the road to school, but I opened it when I got it anyway. It was hard to read. It seemed like the fakest thing in the world, filled with little clichés and best wishes for my future, like things she cribbed from a touching mother/ daughter movie. A few times it crossed my mind that maybe it *wasn't* fake, but that thought made me feel strangely guilty and sad. I tried reading it a second time, but it got too hard. I put it in the ziplock bag with the other stuff.

"You going to make it, rock star?" asked Mike when he came to say good-bye a few days before I was due to leave. I was lying in the backyard on a lawn chair, holding on to one end of Superhero's drooly wet rope toy.

"I'm nervous," I said. "But I think I'm more nervous now that I know what happened last year. I'm more nervous about that happening again than going to school."

"But at least you know you don't want that to happen," said Mike. "You didn't know that was even a possibility last time, right?"

"Yeah," I said.

"Just don't fall in love with someone at another school," he said. "Starting freshman year late is probably a pain, but nothing is as big a bitch as transferring."

Then the day came. The drive back east to Ohio felt exactly the same as the same drive last year. We even stopped at the same Arby's in Indiana that we had on the way back. I had the roast beef. I contemplated getting something different, to signify a change in my life, but thought that that would be kind of dumb.

"Cecily . . ." Dad said when we got back in the car. I was driving this time.

"Yeah?" I asked. I was feeling jittery. I didn't know if it was the huge Coke I'd had or just run-of-the-mill nervousness.

"How are you feeling?"

"Fine," I said.

"Cecily?" he said. "I just want to say . . ." and he coughed. "I don't know that I've always made the best decisions. And it kills me to think that I might have . . . I don't know, done something not right for you. So I want you to know . . ." and he coughed again. Jesus Christ, it was excruciating. "I want you to know that all I wanted was to make you happy."

"Okay," I said. "Thanks, Dad." I didn't know what else to say. "Do you mind if I put on the radio?" I didn't feel like talking any more.

"Sure," he said.

We got to campus and pulled into the parking lot, where, once again, a sea of incoming freshmen carried garbage bags, boxes, and laundry baskets. Their hopeful mothers carried vacuum cleaners and irons that would probably never be used. For the hell of it, I'd brought the poster that Mom had given me at Christmas. I figured I'd let Lauren decide if it should go up or if it should be banished under the bed.

"Cecily Powell?" I said when I got to the big picnic table that had the freshmen orientation information. A smiling, squinting girl in a purple NEW STUDENT ORIENTATION! T-shirt with the short sleeves rolled up handed me a small envelope. "Here you go! Room assignment and keys. Welcome!" I heard her fellow orienters saying exactly the same thing, word for word, to the other kids around me.

"Where is it?" Dad asked, trying to get ahold of the student map that was in my packet. He was a sucker for maps.

"It's this way," I said, following one of the campus signs. "Let's go." I hustled off, and he had to run a little bit to catch up. We just had to do this.

*I* had to do this.


We stood in the room. I was in a brand-new dorm, compared to last time, when I was assigned to a room in what looked like a housing project from the 1960s. This place smelled like new carpeting and paint. Not exactly a homey feel, but it smelled like a fresh start. My boxes were piled so high, I could make a fort out of them if I wanted to. That actually might be kind of fun.

"What now?" said Dad. "You want help unpacking? Should we get a bite? Do you want to go down to the parent/freshman mixer? I saw a sign for it."

"No," I said, and shook my head. *This is real*, I thought. *This is not a drill.*

"You okay?" asked Dad, and put his arm around my shoulders. For a second, I felt tears welling up inside me. Or were they in him? I couldn't tell exactly.

"Yeah," I said, and shrugged out from under his arm. "You should go."

"Nah, it's okay," he said. "I can help you."

"No really," I said. "I mean it. Time to go."

"Are you Cecily?" I heard a voice behind me, loud and Southern. I'd probably find it grating after a few days, but I planted a big smile on my face and turned around.

# acknowledgments (in reverse alphabetical order)

My parents, Ed and Janice Zulkey, for always supporting me as a writer and pushing me to work as hard as I could at everything.

Julie Strauss-Gabel. I never got why other writers spent so much time lionizing their editors in their acknowledgments, but I get it now. Thank you for taking a chance on me and believing in this project and for all your wonderful hard work and the good conversations. It's been such a pleasure working with you.

Liz McArdle, for being one of the best things ever to come from my college experience, for being a great, supportive friend, and of course for her insight into the world of college admissions. Being your freshman-year roommate was totally worth it.

My agent, Byrd Leavell, for persistently believing in me and also blowing sunshine up my butt only when appropriate.

Stevie Kuenn and Jim Norton, for the Madison color and copyediting mark translation.

John Green, for introducing me to Julie Strauss-Gabel, but also for being a good friend, talented individual, lovely guy, cheerleader, and cohost. I'm proud to know you.

Nora Geraghty, for her long-distance evaluation of Cecily's situation, offering expertise in the world of child psychology, and for being a great old friend.

Lucy Chambers, for the good edits.

Andy Behrens, Will Leitch, Kristen Pettit, and Melissa Walker for giving me insight into YA writing.

AND: Julie Friedman, Lindsay Robertson, Kelly Mulvaney, Wendy McClure, E. Jean Carroll, Keith Phipps, Nathan Rabin, Whitney Pastorek, Dave Reidy, Mike Sacks, Kevin Guilfoile, Miles Harvey, Sandi Wisenberg, Jessica Riddle, John Sagan, and all the Pie People out there.

## about the author

Like Cecily, Claire Zulkey did everything you're *supposed* to do before graduating high school, if a little more intensely: she attended an SAT class, took the SATs a second time to improve her math score, had a private college counselor, and applied to ten schools before choosing Georgetown University.

While *An Off Year* is a work of fiction, Claire drew on some real-life experiences: she did have a private college admissions coach; she got into her first choice (Georgetown), despite having had a similarly named classmate's transcript submitted instead of her own; and, like her character Kate, Claire's freshman year roommate was a New Yorker named Liz, but the real Liz's accent wasn't fake and she did not bring beer with her when she moved into the room.

Since graduating in 2001, Claire has written for such publications as WallStreetJournal.com, the *Chicago Tribune*, *ElleGirl*, *Modern Bride*, and the Huffington Post and received her Masters in Creative Writing from Northwestern University and has decided that she is done with school for a while. An early blogger, she is also the creator of Zulkey.com, which has been featured in the *New Yorker*, *USA Today*, and on Anderson Cooper 360°.